Kei

Erni Aladjai
Translated from the Indonesian by
Nurhayat Indriyatno Mohamed

 Dalang Publishing

Kei

Originally published as *Kei* in 2013 by GagasMedia, Jakarta, Indonesia (ISBN: 10-979-780-649-9 and 13-978-979-780-649-1)

Copyright © 2013 Erni Aladjai

Translation copyright © 2014 Nurhayat Indriyatno Mohamed

Publication of this book is subsidized by the Center for Research and Development, Office of Research and Development, Ministry of Education and Culture of the Republic of Indonesia, and in collaboration with Penerbit PT Gramedia Pustaka Utama.

Cover design by Robert Kato
Book design by Son Do
Editor: Sal Glynn
Indonesian literary advisor: Manneke Budiman

Dalang Publishing LLC
San Mateo, CA
www.dalangpublishing.com
dalangpublishing@gmail.com

ISBN: 978-0-9836273-6-4
Library of Congress number: 2014950615

KEI

Map of Indonesia

N
W
E
S
Pacific
Ocean
Sulawesi
Irian
Barat
Ambon
Makassar
Banda Sea
Kei
Islands
Arafura Sea

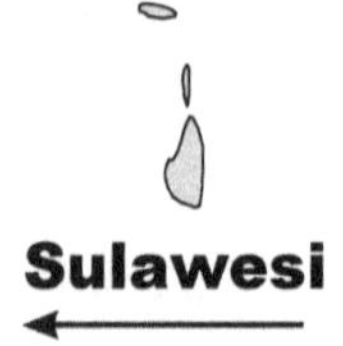

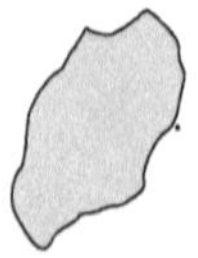

Sulawesi

Banda Sea

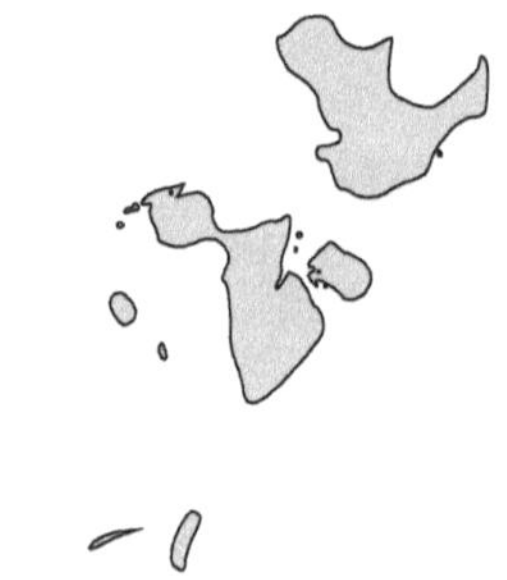

Map of Kei Islands

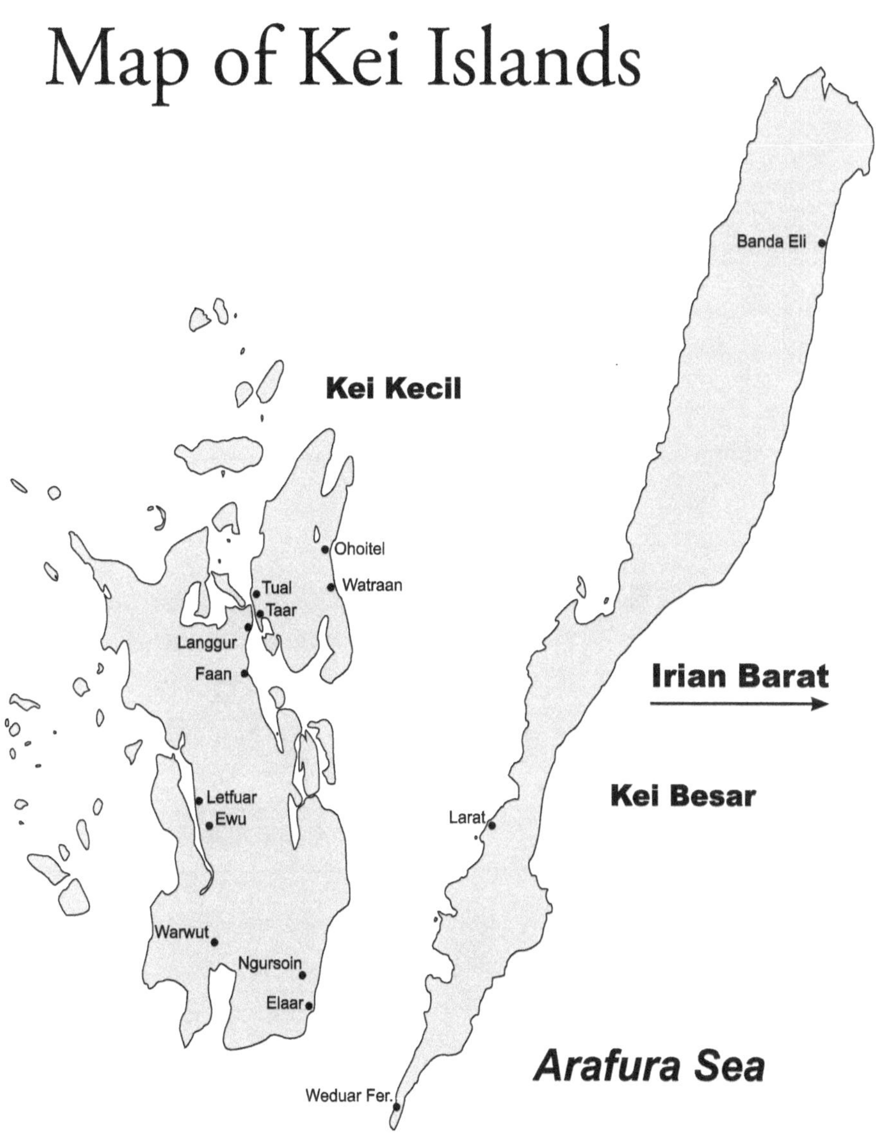

Translator's Note

As a news editor, I value accuracy in a story above all else: the names, events, dates, and places. Putting these pieces together in the right order gives the reader a clear perspective of what happened.

The chance to translate *Kei* by Erni Aladjai into English seemed ideal for me, the boy-meets-girl story set amid a conflict that happened only a few years ago and was comprehensively covered by the local press.

But once I got into the process of translating, I realized the conflict in Maluku was less complete than I thought. The popular narrative about a Muslim-Christian conflict belied the true complexity of the event. No news reports spoke of Christians sheltering Muslim refugees in their churches, or the reverence the people of Kei had for their ancestral beliefs—more so than the imported religions in whose names they were whipped into a murderous frenzy.

No news features appeared about the families and communities torn apart by the conflict and forced to flee their ancestral homes, or the values that helped some communities survive and grow again.

The news media is great with facts, but falls short when it comes to color. *Kei* fills in the missing color by lighting up the dark corners and drawing attention to the bright spots. The main character, Namira Evav, is one of thousands of people affected by the conflict. To say their fate was the same as hers would be grossly inaccurate and unfair, yet Namira's story illustrates the ordeals experienced by the ordinary Kei islander whose world was turned upside down by the events of that period.

Erni Aladjai has done a wonderful job conjuring the details of Kei culture for an audience largely ignorant of its wisdoms, even here in Indonesia. My challenge was to translate the colors so they retained the luster and vibrancy of the original, and I believe—with help from the very determined publisher, Lian Gouw, and accomplished and diligent editor, Sal Glynn—I have managed to do just that.

Nurhayat Indriyatno Mohamed
May 2014

KEI

Between 1999 and 2001, some 9,700 people were reported killed, 1,000 permanently injured, 17,000 women lost their husbands, 15,000 people lost their jobs and 321,473 people were forced to flee because of sectarian violence in Maluku.

—from *Laskar Jihad: Kambing Hitam Konflik Maluku* (*Laskar Jihad: the Black Sheep of the Maluku Conflict*) by Mohammad Shoelhi (Jakarta: Pustaka Zaman, 2002)

Chapter 1

Port of Makassar, South Sulawesi, November 2001

Namira Evav found herself trapped in the commotion of thousands of passengers. A cacophony of vendors sold dusty fruit and passion fruit juice, and rice boxes with the rice half-cooked and a barely cooked chicken wing. She carried a bag tinted the gray of a Java sparrow.

As soon as the ship *Bukit Siguntang* docked, the passengers scrambled for the stairs. Namira joined the rush. She raced against the others, squeezing between porters carrying sacks and large boxes. Fortunately, her tiny frame allowed her to weave through the throng, sliding past people. It was worse on the stairs. The porters pushed past the women and children. Namira was stuck until she emerged from the crowd into a corridor on the deck. After going up and down the stairs, she broke into a smile when she saw an empty space at the end of the fourth deck.

She spread out the used paper cement sack she had bought for five hundred rupiah from a teenager with a pierced ear. She had to occupy the spot before anyone else. Many of the passengers slept in the ship's hold or on the open deck, having failed to find space in the corridors.

She was twenty years old. Time could stretch or shrink; it could teach forgiveness. It could revive love and quell hatred.

***

For Namira, coming home was like celebrating her memories: poached mackerel with steamed *enbal* on the dining table covered with an orange cloth, the crash of the waves, the rustling of palm trees, and the fire consuming the whole island. The purple *roro* flowers scattered on the beach, love that hurt, a ritual by the sea, sounds of gunfire and explosions, and fear that had vanished.

On the flight of stairs in front of her, people climbed up and down to the deck. They came and went. Namira had lost her home a long time ago. For a long time she felt uprooted, homeless. That was until Mery Kaplale, her best friend in grade school, phoned her one afternoon. She asked her to return to the island of Kei Kecil. Mery needed her.

"No matter what, Kei is still your home. The people need you. I want you to work with me. Come back for Kei. I'll be waiting for you," Mery pleaded. She hung up before Namira could answer.

Mery was a Catholic girl with long curly hair, brown skin, and a loud, carefree laugh. She had hugged Namira in front of a refugee camp two years earlier in Langgur, across the bridge south of Tual. It was a month before she boarded the freight ship, *Cinta Semusim,* bound for Makassar. She had evacuated along with the Buginese, Makassarese, and Buton people going back to their homelands after their stores and stalls had burned.

Along with her Uncle Orlando, Mery had traveled a great distance to track down Namira. They visited dozens of islands by motorboat as the conflict rose in Southeast Maluku, looking for news of her. Namira's eyes watered.

"You still love me, even if I am a Muslim?" she had asked Mery.

"There is no Muslim or Christian, Ra. We are all the same. We eat from the same plate and we sleep together, but the conflict has separated us." As she thought of Mery's words, a tear rolled down Namira's face. Her vision blurred.

That afternoon her mind was like a roll of film, playing back the past. She remembered conversations, and the sadness and happiness that once was. Two weeks before she had said goodbye to Kumala. She and Mery were like sisters to her.

"So where are you going, Ra?" Kumala had asked.

"Kei Island, I am going home."

"Where is that?"

"Between the Banda Sea and the Arafura Sea."

Kumala frowned and asked for an explanation.

"In Southeast Maluku, Tual."

Namira showed Kumala the small map she always carried, a hand-drawn gift from Mery. She smiled when she thought of how Mery had treated her like a tourist when in fact she was born in Kei and the island was her heaven. Her eyes turned misty recalling Mery's note on the back of the map, "Bring this in case you forget the way home."

Kumala, who was fond of painting, had not been able to picture the location of Kei Island. She had looked at the map almost with despair.

"Here, look, in this part," Namira said, drawing a straight line with her finger.

"Mmm, that is really far, Ra. I heard there is still fighting on your island."

Namira ended the conversation with, "No matter what, it is my home."

She settled on the paper sack, took a can of soda pop from a plastic bag, and drank without a straw. Kumala had always said that a woman looked sexy when she threw back her drinks. Heaven only knew where she got the idea.

On her journey of hundreds of miles, Namira had an unrecognizable feeling. The conflict had not made her forget about Kei, not really. Her sadness of going home was linked with the difficulty in accepting her parents' death. Her mother's burial place remained a mystery. Was it at a mosque that was burned? At a church that was burned? On the road? In the sea? In the forest?

Namira tucked the small map in her backpack. Mery had drawn it with love. Now the map would lead her home.

***

She had barely taken her first gulp of soda pop when the ship's whistle blew for the third time. It was like the ringing of a church bell. The anchor was raised as the ship readied to leave the port. *Bukit Siguntang* set sail beneath a wet November sky.

A name in the back of her mind suddenly jumped to the foreground: Sala. She had buried that name for too long. He was the only man who provoked a sense of longing in her. His teachings about the old ways of Kei and care for their land still rang in her ears.

One by one, the lines came back. She echoed each verse he had uttered, like a student memorizing a prayer:

> *We inhabit a village where we live and*
> *eat from the land.*
> *We occupy a place that is ours and protect*
> *what is ours.*
> *We uphold all that is important for the*
> *village with the traditional laws.*
> *We live as honestly as we can and stand*
> *upright as we move forward.*
> *Thus, the traditions will protect us*
> *So that our ancestors also protect us*
> *And God will bless us.*

Where was the man with his strong belief in tradition? Was he in the forest? At sea? Or in the village of Watraan? The vision of a gravestone with his name flashed before her. Namira closed her eyes and shook her head. "No, I'll see him again. That is certain."

Namira would be happy if he had found another woman, just as long as God still protected him. She exhaled. Her journey to Kei was like searching for the home of an old friend who had died in a crowded city; she had been there, but forgotten the road signs.

She had almost forgotten the way back home. She was still too sad to remember what happened two years ago in the villages of Elaar, Ohoinol, Langgur, and Evu. Her sadness resembled a funeral on a rainy day, and her memories were too tragic. In the end, she was in the belly of the ship with her mind moving back and forth. Her memories were a wound that had not healed. An abscess of distrust, fear, and pain festered in her heart. She had not quite forgotten everything, yet she remained a stranger to her own past.

Chapter 2

Elaar, Kei Kecil, March 1999

Namira took off her *biljab*. Water from her ablutions still clung to her face. She hurriedly hung the veil and her mat on a nylon string stretching from the doorjamb to the corner of the window in her room. She had just finished her afternoon prayer. Her face was radiant and flushed, the color of a tomato.

Namira loved everything about Elaar. The mountain, the long stretch of white sandy beach, the sound of breaking waves, the coral reef, the boats, the full moon glinting on the sea, and the whistling of conch shells on magical nights, was like the flapping of a fairy's wings.

Elaar was in the south of Kei Kecil. To Namira, Elaar was a hidden fairy village, inaccessible to big city tourists for whom the journey was too far. Those who had visited and enjoyed Kei Beach said it was further than flying from London to Moscow.

Namira swayed softly in her room, her hands twirling. Her feet moved to a rhythm. The floorboards creaked beneath her. She practiced the *Sosoy Swar Man-Vuun* dance, stopping to crane her head to the window now and again. Outside, a crowd made their way to the beach. She looked at those passing by.

Will Mery come or not, she wondered. Namira moved from the window. She retreated like a turtle hiding from a predator, and stepped back even further. She paced her room, waiting for the friend she loved like a sister.

The walls of her room were made of planks. A poster with the *Ayatul Kursi,* or Throne Verse, from the Qur'an was tacked on the wall. Near it hung a mirror in a carved leaf frame, and next to the mirror was a calendar with the picture of an Angora cat, its eyes as clear as lake water. The cat nestled in a wicker basket lined with a soft-looking fabric. On the other side of the calendar was another poster cut from an almanac. It showed the actress Diana Pungky in a bright green sleeveless dress and a yellow bandana carrying a basket of ripe cacao pods.

Namira moved to the mirror, its glass clouded with dust wafted in by the sea breeze. She pulled in closer until her face was just an inch away from the mirror. Her eyes were the brown of coral, her eyebrows thick and neat. Her hair was wavy, her nose aquiline. People said that her toast-like complexion and strong nose were beauty traits passed down from her grandmother, who came from the Makian Timur clan—descendants of Arabs and Malays on the island of Ternate—while her hair and eyebrows were from her grandfather, a full-blooded Bandanese.

Namira picked up a jar of face powder with a picture of a mother and a chubby-cheeked baby on the label. She poured some powder into her hand and applied a thin layer on her face. She looked at her white *kebaya*, almost the color of a nutmeg flower, and pinned a fish brooch made of seashell to her breast. She smiled, content.

***

The *Tutup Sasi Laut* ceremony would be held that day in Elaar. Two days earlier, Namira had entrusted a letter to a traveling salesman who had come through Elaar on his way to Evu, in the center of Kei Kecil. Namira had sent an invitation to Mery to join the Sosoy Swar Man-Vuun dance in Elaar. Namira wrung her hands. A shrill voice called her name from the other side of the gate. "Ra, are you ready? I came over with Uncle Orlando."

Namira peered out the window. Mery looked beautiful in her clean, white kebaya. Around her neck, she wore a necklace with a silver cross pendant that glinted in the sunlight. She waved her handkerchief in the air, laughing. Her Uncle Orlando had brought her over on his motorboat, just so she could be with Namira in Elaar.

The two young women walked hand in hand to the Tutup Sasi Laut ceremony.

Everyone had already gathered when they reached the beach. The heady smell of cheap perfume high in alcohol content rose from the crowd.

For the people of Kei, the Sasi Laut was like the words in the Holy Book. The rules were supposed to prevent people from breaking the customary laws. In Elaar, the tribal elders, nobles, and land barons—more like priests than landowners— ensured the traditional regulations on land were kept.

The Sasi Laut observed in Elaar that day, prohibited people from harvesting sea cucumbers before the time determined by tradition. On the islands of Kei Kecil and Kei Besar, fishing with dynamite, cyanide, or fine-meshed nets was prohibited.

The previous night young people walked through the village blowing into conch shells, heralding the Sasi Laut ritual. It marked the end of a two-week period in which everyone stocked up on food. The men salted and smoked fish, because once the Sasi Laut was closed, no one was allowed to fish.

***

Namira and Mery heard the commotion by the time they reached the edge of the beach. All the older villagers appeared to be busy with the Sasi Laut ceremony. Amid the bustle, young people practiced playing *tifa* drums beneath the palm trees.

To the north, a pair of sea eagles flew low, darting at schools of fish before soaring above the crowd. An older man gave a serious-sounding interview to a reporter from Ambon, not far from where the girls stood.

"Our traditional ceremony regulates the exploitation of natural resources from the island. Tutup Sasi forbids the harvesting of sea cucumbers for six months. It also prohibits anyone from disturbing the marine ecosystem. This gives living creatures time to grow and reproduce, and protects the ecosystem. All the Kei islands have a Tutup Sasi ritual. This is how we show respect for the sea, because our livelihood comes from the sea."

"What's the punishment for violating this tradition, *pak*?" the reporter asked.

The man paused for a moment, and then said firmly: "Anyone who violates the law will suffer an unspeakable shame."

Namira heard snatches of the conversation carried by the breeze. She recalled a time when she was eleven years old. The memory made her shudder. Her uncle Uar had lived next door. He was single and often brought her seashells. She strung the shells to make bracelets, which she sometimes gave to him.

Uncle Uar lived alone. The crawlspace beneath his house was littered with clamshells and had a rank odor. There were also fish traps, nets, and a boat that needed repair.

Once he violated the Tutup Sasi. He had picked a sea cucumber before the time set by the traditional law. The tribal chief and council of the elders punished Uncle Uar. He had to carry his own excrement around the village while shouting, "I'm no good for this village. I'm as good as this excrement."

It had saddened Namira to watch Uncle Uar carry his own excrement and hear his quavering voice. She pulled at her mother's sarong to urge her back inside the house.

Namira's sadness at the sight was the same as when her pet goat—an animal she loved and nursed when it was sick, fed and checked its pen when it rained—had been slaughtered at the mosque on *Eid al-Adha*, the Feast of the Sacrifice.

Uncle Uar walked by, his body stooped and reeking of excrement. For the duration of the punishment, everyone had to stand outside and watch as Uncle Uar staggered under his burden. His relatives cried from shame. But this was the Kei tradition. It had to be done or the people would suffer the wrath of their ancestors. When the violation was announced, Uncle Uar's clan name was also clearly mentioned, making his private infraction a reflection of the family's conduct. That was why every individual and family tried as best they could to abide by the traditional laws. It was for the good of their own reputation, good standing, and the honor of their family.

The next day at sunset, Uncle Uar was found facedown in a hedge of *kecubung*. It appeared he had been so ashamed that he ground the seeds and consumed them until he was intoxicated. A villager who lived near the hedge said Uncle Uar had shouted all afternoon, lamenting his crime.

***

The ceremony proceeded in silence. The tribal chief tied a palm frond to a wooden pole anchored in the sea off the beach. The gesture meant the prohibition on sea cucumbers had come into force. People would only be allowed to gather them again when the frond was untied.

The ritual was over and Mery, Namira, and the other girls of Elaar performed the Sosoy Swar Man-Vuun dance for those in attendance. Rustling palm leaves mingled with the rhythm of the drums. Fans carried by the dancers flapped in the sea breeze. Everyone was carefree.

But the festive atmosphere of celebration to show respect for nature was suddenly silenced. A young man on a Yamaha motorbike rode into the crowd. He had news: an attack was coming. A sense of dread descended on hearing the news from the unknown source. No one spoke. Everyone looked at each other and wiped their faces.

Sensing the panic, the deputy bishop of Amboina, an invited guest to the Tutup Sasi, stepped forward. He said, "No one must take any sides. Catholics, Protestants, and Muslims—no one need to get involved in the conflict."

Ismael Kabalmay, the imam of the mosque in Elaar, agreed with the deputy. "We should not get involved. Whether you are a Kei, or a Buginese, Papuan, Javanese, Makassarese, or Buton migrant, we are all brothers and sisters. Here our religious differences are not a reason for hatred."

Everyone was asked to embrace, and Namira and Mery hugged each other tight. Around them, the crowd asked how to keep the village safe. Mery and Namira headed for the edge of the beach. The rustle of palm leaves now gave a sense of foreboding. Thoughts about what would happen next consumed them.

"We're still sisters, Mery," Namira said in a hushed voice.

Much embracing happened that day, and worry and fear.

After the ritual, Namira and the people of Elaar went on with their lives. But they could not shake their apprehension.

***

The roofs of the houses, the dirt roads, and the surface of the sea were awash in the light of the Wednesday afternoon sun. Clouds in the east bunched into the shape of a bowl. On the pier, a group of children played. Namira waved at them.

She walked to the other end of the village for the sago her father had finished crushing. He had gone to check on their sago palms two weeks earlier. The leaves had yellowed and the buds began to sprout. The starchy fiber was dense from the trunk to the branches; those were the signs the sago was ready to cut down. It was eight years old.

Namira thought of her mother's retelling of a legend as she walked, about the baby girl whose body was covered with scabs. The baby had been abandoned. When she grew older and could scratch herself, the scabs fell off her legs, arms, and neck, and turned into plants. Later, her mother said, people gave the plants a name: the sago palm.

The shady, wet, and humid road to the jungle was always empty. On the left of the footpath leading to the sago farm was an estuary with clear water. Dozens of dragonflies skimmed its surface. Namira knew dragonflies were the sign of a clean environment.

She went down to the river and washed her face. Some years ago, a group from Jakarta came to this river. They stirred up the sediment looking for mica or quartz. Within a month of the monetary crisis breaking out, they were gone.

After a fifteen-minute walk, Namira recognized the acidic odor of the sago. Only the felled trunks were left. In time, they would attract hordes of red palm beetles that laid their larvae inside. Fat white maggots would emerge, and many villagers collected them to make curry. Namira could never eat the sago maggots even knowing they had high protein content and no cholesterol. It gave her the creeps to think of them wriggling and throbbing.

As sunset approached, Namira walked back to the village carrying a basket of sago. Sounds of a commotion grew more distinct the nearer she got to the village. There was swearing and cursing. Namira took a step back. As far as she could see, strangers wielded machetes, sharpened sticks, and guns. Light bounced off machete blades and spear tips, and made her dizzy. Fear gripped her heart and pinned her feet to the ground.

The sound of a gunshot pierced the air.

"Letfuar and Ngursoin have come for us. Run and hide in the forest," a young man shouted. Two neighboring villages were invading Elaar. Namira's knees shook. The machetes of the men storming her village were splashed with blood. They had just carried out a massacre. The thudding of bare feet on the ground churned up a cloud of dust as they hunted for those not on their side.

Namira felt weak, as though all her bones were disjointed. Hysteria gripped the villagers. Calls roared through the air like the noise of a helicopter's propellers.

Mothers, in-laws, friends, lovers, children, husbands, grandmothers and grandfathers, and siblings howled for each other in the chaos. People scrambled from their homes. The village became even more frantic. Families split apart and scattered.

Less than a week before, people broke into cold sweats on hearing news of the attack and slaughter by the Dayaks against the Madurese settlements in West Kalimantan. Not a day went by without more bloodshed on television screens and front pages of the newspapers. Was today Kei's turn?

Namira's thoughts were a blur. Why did such conflicts always start with the mischief of young men? Were they paid to spark unrest? Did someone with unimaginable power plan this?

She felt as if she had fireflies in her eyes. Namira put down the basket of sago she carried. Her body almost collapsed but her heart told her to find her father in the forest. Her heart willed it, yet her nerves would not respond. Her feet remained frozen.

Not far from where she stood, a man in a yellow shirt and gray trousers lay on the road. Blood trickled from the back of his head to stain the asphalt beneath him.

A few meters from the body, a man held a jerry can. He splashed its contents on a young man who ran past him. The stinging smell of kerosene hit Namira as the man with the jerry can sparked a lighter. Flames consumed the bodies of the innocent. Everywhere was the odor of singed hair. Namira suddenly felt sick. She vomited on the road.

She screamed until her voice went hoarse. Her legs refused to move until a stranger pulled her by the arm. Her skinny frame squeezed into the crowd heading for the forest. They would seek shelter in the next village. It was still dusk. By sundown, they had been driven from their own village.

The survivors from Elaar pressed on through the dense forest. Their bodies itched from the poisonous plants and the spiky brush of wild pineapples scratched their shins. They walked with tears in their eyes as the sky gradually became darker, toward Ohoinol, a farming village in the eastern district of Kei Kecil.

The locals met Namira and the other refugees, and sheltered them inside the village church. There was no religious segregation. Muslim refugees packed into the church, guarded by the Catholic residents of Ohoinol. They kept the peace and protected their Muslim and Protestant brethren. Namira huddled in a corner of the church, sobbing.

By daybreak, the number of refugees had increased. A gray-haired man with gold-rimmed glasses moved to the center of the mass of people lost in their thoughts. It was Father Fritz. Namira knew him well.

When she was in grade school, her father had often asked her to take fresh fish over to Father Fritz's house. Sometimes when the church held a charity event, her father had helped set up the tent.

Father Fritz looked at the drained faces. He gripped the shoulder of a young man who had lost his wife, trying to give him strength. A moment later, he said in Kei dialect:

"We are all brothers. We are all eggs hatched from the same fish and the same bird.

"Let us never forget the wisdom of our ancestors. We come from one line. All Kei people are brothers and sisters."

The priest's words rekindled the refugees' spirits. They embraced and shared their food, blankets, and medicines.

Chapter 3

Sala gasped in front of the bamboo gate painted white and blue. His blood seemed to stop coursing through his veins. Fifteen minutes earlier, he had heard a group of people shouting, the cries piercing the searing heat of Watraan. The *musim kemarau*, or dry season, had come sooner than expected. Tongues of fire reached high into the sky. They spread fast, thanks to the weather and sea breeze. Black smoke filled the sky.

From the south came gunshots followed by an explosion, and then wailing. People with looks of despair wound through the village streets like ants returning to the colony. They carried all the household goods they could take with them.

Children screamed for their mothers and fathers. As he watched the attackers advance into the village, Ahmad

Udfan, a fisherman who lived a little more than fifty yards from Sala's house, picked up his machete. He jumped in front of one of the blood-crazed attackers. The clang of blades made it apparent to Sala: Kei was in upheaval.

Pots, pans, and basins flew into yards as though a tornado had struck. The attackers tossed everything out of the homes. They burned chairs, tables, and cupboards. People's prized possessions were set ablaze as though lighting a bonfire of dried leaves. The smell of burning resin was pungent and heady.

In the aftermath of an explosion, a man emerged carrying the body of his wife. A son carried the body of his father. Another carried his wounded mother. A young man carried his shell-shocked lover. Bodies littered the street, covered in banana leaves.

The villagers who survived were weighed down with anguish. They had been banished from their own land.

The young children of Kei, accustomed to hearing the crashing of the waves, were assaulted by the different sounds of an explosion, gunfire, and screaming. The villagers of Kei Kecil, once at peace with their different religions, were now divided into two parts, Muslim and Christian. The Whites and the Reds. One side wore white bandanas, the other red.

***

Sala had returned that afternoon from delivering knives to a group of women on Mun Kahar, a small island off Kei Besar. They often bought the knives his mother made and sold them at the market. From the sea, he could see fires and black smoke creeping to the south of the village. The smoke drifted west and covered the red-tiled roofs of the villagers' homes. He knew the violence had come to Watraan.

He revved the engine of his boat. Cold sweat trickled down his face. Whatever was happening in Watraan was sudden and unexpected.

Sala's legs felt weak. He cried without knowing, his eyes stinging as though a fistful of pepper were rubbed into them. His chest was tight. In the front yard, his mother lay face down across the cacao seeds left out to dry. The bell-shaped banana flower she recently planted had fallen over. She had watered it that morning while singing, "*Olesio sayange, rasa sayang, sayange…*"

Blood flowed on the orange tarp used to spread the cacao seeds, and stained her white clothes. When Sala left the house, his mother was steaming enbal and cooking fish curry. Just as he was about to go out the door she had called from the kitchen, "Hurry home. May God and the ancestors guard you on your journey."

The people of Kei always invoked God and their ancestors in their prayers and wishes. Before the major religions arrived, it was just the ancestors.

She also told Sala to have lunch at home and watch the drying cacao to make sure it was not eaten or kicked around by ducks and chickens.

Sala cried at the memory. His mother hated to see a man cry, but the tears came from his loss. Everyone grieved and now it was his turn. His mother lay dead before him.

He picked up the body and carried her inside the house. Martina, the Kei woman who had brought up her son alone in her own tough way, was gone. He put her down on the wooden recliner.

Sala felt incredibly lonely. He cleaned the blood from Martina's sinewy arms. Her rigid face looked innocent. Through the years, she had made a life for them in any way she could. She cut down sago trees; she sold enbal in Tual, going by motorboat; she made machetes and knives; she even made *kasbi* bread and sold it around the village. She was a tough woman.

After the visit of President B.J. Habibie, violence had flared on the islands of Haruku and Saparua. The refugees fled to the Kei islands, where the conflict soon grew out of control.

***

Martina had introduced Sala to fire, knives, and machetes. Since the age of five, he had stayed by her side when she forged the blades. She was good at metalworking. Her father, La Kape, had been a skilled blacksmith from the Tukangbesi islands off the southeastern tip of Sulawesi. He moved to Watraan and married Maria Renwarin, a sweet Protestant girl. La Kape renounced his faith for Maria and became a devout Protestant, a loving husband, a diligent churchgoer, and a willing helper for his neighbors.

La Kape had hoped the machetes would help him make a living and spent long hours learning to become a master blacksmith. Maria, Martina's mother, was good at cooking and massage. When Martina was little, many people came by asking her mother to give them a massage. She traded her skills for a bottle of coconut oil, clams, sago, or cassava.

Martina's parents had been killed on Seram Island during a battle between the South Maluku Republic and the Indonesian military. Stray bullets hit the couple as they went around selling knives. They had begun and ended their lives together.

Martina had waited the entire day for them in the doorway of her father's workshop. Her parents never came home. From that time, Martina dedicated herself to keeping the workshop running.

Every day she made knives and machetes for customers from Ternate to the Tanimbar islands, but the fire in the workshop's furnace had gone out that afternoon. No tempering or red-hot embers of coal. A shadow descended over the house.

Sala bathed his mother's body. His eyes were red as he soaped her arms. The same arms that had forged blades for years were now still.

He prepared the grave as the sun set behind the leaves of the *noni* tree, digging until his fingers and nails turned black. Sala buried his mother at the foot of the tree. He was wracked by grief different from any funeral he had attended, for there was no priest, church, or coffin. No eulogy for the deceased, no one wearing black. There was only him, alone.

A bottle took the place of a headstone. Rocks and wild grasses bordered the grave missing a name, date of birth, or date of death. Sala sat by the grave for days until a neighbor led him back home. "Stop mourning for your mother. It will not bring her back. Go home. Honor her by being a man who is tough, who works, and who can survive the loneliness. It's no good moping by the grave for too long."

Sala went home to find it cloaked in sadness. The firewood was lonely. The kitchen herbs were dry and the water jars cloudy with mosquito larvae. The plates were dusty. His mother, who took care of those household chores, was gone.

He walked through the house. His only neighbor, the woman who urged him to go home, had quickly evacuated. The living had abandoned the village once the dead were buried. Sala was alone.

The wavy haired young man looked at the sideboard with the cloudy mirror leaning against the wall. One of its legs was shorter than the others and propped up with a block. Sala took out the tea set of fine china that belonged to his mother. She had loved the cups, saucers, and teapot the most after her workshop, because they were all she had left of her father and mother.

When Sala was little, his mother had almost sold the tea set before Christmas Eve. She was sad she could not buy him new clothes to wear in church for the midnight mass. She cried when she put the tea set on the bed.

These old items are worth more than anything else in this house, but my son is the most precious of all.

She stared at the white porcelain and stroked the pieces one by one with her dark hand: the graceful curve of the teapot's spout, the hand-painted lotus and wren motif, and the *fenghuang* adorning the bowl. Martina's eyes glazed over. When her father and mother were hiding from Dutch soldiers during the fight for independence, they found a hole containing the set.

Sala saw his mother's sadness as he peered through the curtain hanging in the doorway. He could not bear to see his mother sad. He returned the pieces to the sideboard. "*Beta* does not want new clothes, Mama. I can wear my old clothes."

Martina hugged Sala. She kissed him repeatedly. Now more than a dozen years later, Sala took down the set. He wrapped each piece in a rag and put them inside a large saucepan with a dent in one corner.

He took the pan into the backyard and dug a hole in the ground. Sala buried the saucepan inside, sticking a machete handle in the ground to mark the spot so he could find it again. He promised that once the village was safe, he would return to his house.

Being alone in the house made him sad. He was nineteen on the day his mother died. Only a year ago he was wearing a high school uniform. Sala had imagined he would study in the city of Ambon, at Pattimura University. He wanted to study mechanical engineering and join Matepala, the engineering school's environmental club.

When he was in middle school, he hiked twice with university students from the Matepala club. They climbed Mount Binaiya, the mountain that formed the island of Seram, and the tallest in Maluku. It was said that the mountain was a stairway to the clouds. In daylight, it was difficult to see the top because clouds obscured the view. The peak was only visible at daybreak.

Sala had also climbed Mount Daab by himself. It was almost 3000 feet tall, the highest on Kei Kecil.

During the climb, he met local elders and officials. A standoff was taking place. The Southeast Maluku Forestry Department had driven piles into the ground around the mountain, without letting the tribal elders know. The piles had to do with a group of people who arrived later to explore the area for oil, as well as inquire about the ironwood and sandalwood trees growing around the mountain.

Sala's plans for the future were in tatters. After the death of his mother, nothing was left for him on the island.

***

The women and children were evacuated, and the young and old men of Watraan returned on certain nights. They came out of refuge to gather their meager forces.

On Monday night, March 29, the talk inside the copra warehouse owned by the village chief started in whispers and grew to roars. The warehouse had clapboard walls and a cracked concrete floor. An oil lamp made from a milk can and set on a wooden table was the only light. The flame sputtered each time there was a draft. Laid out on the table were spears, machetes, daggers, and sickles.

Sala looked at the display with anger. What did these men have planned? The talk continued as light from military flares leaked through the gaps in the wall.

Sanan, the village chief, conducted the meeting. His defiance and rage urged the men to retaliate.

"Our village has been torn apart by those savage monsters. You have seen them destroying our property. Those of us who remain must seek vengeance. We must give our attackers what they have given to us," Sanan said.

A cry went up among the men at the chief's call for vengeance. Seated in his chair, Sala explored the corridors of his own conscience.

This desire must be stopped, for reprisal will only make things worse. Death is more than the statistics of corpses. It prolongs the suffering of our village—even if death comes from the hands of those at this meeting.

"Let me apologize beforehand. I realize I'm the youngest at this meeting, but if I may, I would like to offer my opinion." Sala paused for a moment before resuming slowly. "To strike back means we are just like them. What will distinguish us from the attackers if we resort to destruction?"

"Son, can't you see how our brothers, neighbors, and families have been hurt?" Sanan raged.

"Forgive me, gentlemen, if I seem impertinent. I only want to point out the threat to our humanity."

"You are free to leave if you disagree," Sanan said.

Sala rose, excused himself, and walked to the door. The young man shuddered to hear his elders speak of retribution. It was as though they were discussing a plan to build a public toilet. Sala wanted to leave the copra warehouse far behind him.

As the rivers flow into the ocean
But cannot make the vast ocean o'erflow,
So flow the magic streams of the sense-
> *world*
Into the sea of peace that is the sage.

He is forever free who has broken out
Of the ego-cage of I and mine
To be united with the Lord of Love.

The words from Mr. Letsoin, his history teacher, buzzed in Sala's head. It was a quote from the Bhagavad Gita, part of a conversation between Krishna and Arjuna. At the time, Mr. Letsoin was explaining the ancestry of the Kei people, how they originated from a Hindu woman in Bali.

"Go away, young man. For the sake of Watraan, tell no one of our intentions," Sanan said.

Sala turned from the doorway to look at the chief. The pain of a father who lost his child is greater than that of a child who lost his mother, he thought. He too was hurting; he too was angry, but to salve that pain by taking someone else's life was not right.

Middle-aged Ahmad Udfan, whose brother-in-law was killed, watched as Sala disappeared among the palm trees. In his heart, he knew the young man had spoken the truth.

Ahmad volunteered to lead the retaliation. "I know their village as well as my own farm," he said. His daughter, her husband, and their five children lived in the village they planned to attack. He did not want any of them killed.

It made him uneasy to think of the men and weapons involved. "I'll work on the strategy for our entry, exit, and how long we remain in combat."

***

The next night, a team led by Ahmad left the cover of the bushes and walked along the road to the village. They fought fiercely, striking when people were asleep and allowing no time for panic to spread. The sounds of despair, children calling for their mothers and fathers, once again rang out. When Ahmad heard the pleas, he wept. He had told his relatives earlier in the afternoon to leave their home.

Chapter 4

Ohoitel Forest, April 1999

After the attack, Ahmad became a target of the Reds. Not one corner in Watraan could hide him. Those out to get him had the same zeal as the Nazis hunting the Jews.

"Shedding the blood of Ahmad Udfan's lineage is permitted for the next seven generations," decreed a man brandishing a machete in the air.

Ahmad and his family hid amid rocks concealed by lantana plants, a dense grove of trees, and various jungle plants. Sarah, his seven-year-old granddaughter, would not stop crying. They slept crouched on the limestone ground plagued by mosquitoes, and drank turbid water from a crevice in the rocks. The day before, Anton, Ahmad's son-in-law, had stolen into a field and dug up unripe cassava. The tubers were roasted in a gap between the rocks so the smoke would not give them away.

The little girl kept crying. She begged her mother, Sarina, for fried fish and warm rice. She missed her friend's nylon swing, and asked when she would have someone to play with.

Sarina's sister-in-law nursed her youngest child. "Please quiet your child. If they find us, do you think any of us will be left alive?"

Sarina hugged the girl to her breast and stroked her head. "Sarah, why are you crying?"

"I miss Yami and Ruth, Mama," the little girl said, naming her friends.

"Ega, play with Sarah. Go pick some leaves and branches. You can play school or market or whatever."

Ega was two years older than Sarah. She held her cousin's hand and the two girls went off to collect sticks and dried leaves. "These leaves are your money," Ega said. "We'll pretend the twigs are crayons, pencils, and pens, so that when I open a stationery store, you can buy them with the leaf money."

In every war, families at risk found a niche to hide, to protect them from a merciless hunt. Forest, caves, and even ditches were hiding places.

From the top of a hill, the sky was awash in a sea of pink before turning as dark as a heap of ground coffee. One owl, then two, left their holes in the trees. The calls of geckos and lizards caused the children to hide under their mother's armpit. The smallest sound put them on edge. Who knew if it was a python, cobra, or centipede? Ahmad and his son-in-law stayed awake. No one made a campfire. They did not want to do their pursuers any favor.

The women, children, and Ahmad's son-in-law brought their hands to their lips and prayed that those seeking Ahmad would never find their hidden rocky alcove in the forest, home to fifteen souls.

One by one, bodies stretched from the wet grass that for days had been their mattress. The clothes they wore looked bright from being damp.

The sun snuck between the trees. Sarina was first to wake up, and a moment later, she screamed. Sara and Ega were no longer by her side. Panic swept through the group. Where did the children go that early in the morning?

***

The black smoke enveloping Watraan grew thicker, like the gathering of storm clouds before the rain. April became the month of fires.

Sala stood in his doorway, carrying a weathered rucksack filled with clothes. Six of his neighbors had their homes reduced to rubble. The ironwood columns were charred black and the timber frames had crumbled into charcoal. A military camp with two soldiers on guard stood near the ruins. Since the conflict had spread, the government sent help in the form of soldiers from an infantry battalion in Makassar and a company from the Police Mobile Brigade in Bali. Sala felt his heart weep. Where was the Kei bond of brotherhood? His thoughts were confused. Kei was governed by tradition; how could it have succumbed to the conflict?

"One thousand and five hundred years ago, small kingdoms existed on Ambon Island. Charismatic kings ruled, and the people lived in a climate of kinship and pledged allegiance to the Sultanate of Ternate. One day the villagers of Passo and Batu Merah paid a tribute to the Sultan. While returning from Ternate, the boat of the Passo people was overturned by a large wave near Buru Island. They were rescued by the Batu Merah villagers and taken to Tanjung Pela, where they inscribed their blood on a rock. Since that time, the Passo and Batu Merah people have established *pela*, Batu Merah being the older brother and Passo the younger. They pledged that Passo and Batu Merah would never fight or be torn apart." That was the lesson handed down by Mr. Letsoin in their classroom on a hot Tuesday afternoon.

In tumultuous times like these, people should fall back on their history. Sala recalled returning home one afternoon, his face black and blue after getting into a fight with a boy at school who had called him a bastard child.

"Son of a westerner, fatherless son," he said, while his friends looked at Sala in disdain.

Without warning, Sala hurled himself at the boy and punched him in the face. Only after he had split the boy's lip did Sala relent.

As soon as he arrived home, his mother Martina filled a basin with warm water. She applied a warm compress to his temple and bruises. She did not ask questions about what happened. "Son, in the Kei tradition the only reason people fight is to defend the honor of their women and the sanctity of their land. Please do not fight again. A real man does not fight without a good reason."

Sala bowed his head. He felt like less than a man for fighting because of a taunt. *A real man only gets angry when a woman's honor is threatened.* The notion ran through his head. As he grew older, he was convinced he had done the right thing. That boy deserved to be hit for calling him a bastard, because in doing so he had insulted his mother. Sala believed he had fought to defend his mother's honor.

***

The village streets were desolate. Only two houses were unscathed, their doors left wide open after the owners had fled in panic, and held what remained of the village's livestock. The other animals had been burned alive in the carnage.

As Sala passed the military camp, a soldier called out to him. He walked closer.

Five soldiers played cards. One of them mouthed the words to a *dangdut koplo* song coming from inside the tent. Another smoked and looked at Sala with suspicion.

"Where do you come from, *nyong*? Why are you here?"

"Nyong" was a common term of address for young men in Maluku, based on the Dutch word *jong*. The word for a young or unmarried woman was *nona*.

"I'm from this village. My house is near the water tank."

"Where's your family?"

"My family is gone. This conflict has taken everything from us."

"What do you carry in your bag?"

"Clothes, pak."

The soldier threw down his half-finished cigarette. He jerked the rucksack from Sala and searched for concealed weapons: a dagger, poison-tipped arrows, or a grenade. He ordered Sala inside the tent and made him strip to his underwear.

Sala was disgusted when manhandled by the soldier. "I don't have anything illegal."

When the conflict had peaked in Ambon by late January, the local military commander, Major General Amir Sembiring, ordered his men to shoot anyone who carried a weapon and refused to surrender it.

"We'll take you to Langgur. It's still safe there. We can escort you," one soldier said.

"I don't need an escort; I can go on my own. If I die, let me die alone. Escort the women and children."

Another soldier grumbled, "Very cocky, that boy."

"He isn't cocky, just principled."

Sala barely heard them. He kept walking. He was a wanderer, with no one to love or love him.

***

As Watraan succumbed to the fighting, Sala prepared to walk dozens of miles. He entered the forest at the edge of the village and was soon swallowed by dense vegetation. Sala brooded on his grief in the thick brush. The ground beneath his feet was muddy. The further he went, the steeper the ground became. Forest rats darted among ferns and shrubs. Sala had never been afraid of wild animals.

What scared him were people with dark hearts. Toward the afternoon, he reached a rocky slope. His chest ached and his legs were sore. Sweat clouded his vision; he tasted the salt at the corners of his mouth. He exhaled, exhausted, and fell fast asleep.

He spent a troubled night beneath the stars. Wild roosters crowed in the morning, lizards slithered on the branches, parakeets and pythons resumed their search for food, and Sala was thankful. With his strength recovered, he crawled up the slope clinging to exposed tree roots until he reached a path.

Fate placed the unexpected on his path. His heart beat faster at the sight of two little girls before him. They bent over to pick up dried twigs amid the ferns. Were they spirits?

He walked closer and their laughter rang clearly in his ears. The older girl's clothes were wrinkled as though she had worn them for days. One of her legs looked crippled from polio, but her gaze was sharp. The other child had thin, matted red hair, and dirt in the corner of her eyes. Her face was filthy.

Sala approached the children. They bolted. "Wait, kids. Don't run."

They stopped, their eyes wide. "What are your names?"

"Ega."

"Sarah," said the girl with the dirty face and snot-encrusted cheek.

"What are you doing here?"

"Mother says we are hiding from a giant sawfish," said the girl called Sarah, doubt written on her face.

The giant sawfish was a Kei myth. Sala talked with the girls as a rustling in the lantana bushes ahead indicated someone was there. A young man emerged with an arrow in his hand. Sala's throat tightened.

"Who are you?" Anton asked.

"Sala, *pela*." Calling a Maluku man "pela" always calmed his anger.

"You're hiding too?"

"I'm on the run from the fighting in my village."

"Really?"

"Really, pela."

Sala followed him to where Ahmad and his family were hiding. The old man was surprised to see who his son-in-law had brought back. Sarina and Samira rushed to Ega and Sarah.

"Sala."

"Pak Ahmad." Sala was just as surprised to see Ahmad in the middle of the jungle. His fear vanished. Only a few days ago they sat in the copra warehouse, talking about retaliation that Sala refused to join. Ahmad seemed to have aged considerably since then. He welcomed Sala and smiled.

"My family is being chased. Our lives are in danger. We wanted to flee to East Timor, but the situation is even worse than in Kei. They have a war between the Fretilin and the Democratic Union over there."

Sala was silent. He looked around him. How low they had sunk. What had become of them? Five children slept on the mossy ground, wrapped in thin blankets. The women leaned against the trees with wild-eyed stares. Sala wiped his face.

When darkness fell, Sala left the forest and went back to Watraan. He sneaked through his own village, rummaging through abandoned homes with doors left wide open. He looked for blankets, scraps of food, and extra clothes and socks for the children in the forest.

Sala was back in the jungle before sunrise. He handed over the blankets and clothes he had taken from the village. He gave Sarah and Ega a drawing book and colored pencils.

Still shy, the girls took the items and immediately were busy picking out colors. They drew a bird, a sailfish, and a swimming duck.

"That's all I could find. Attackers have burned down most of the houses and destroyed the crops. The village is unsafe and its people are increasingly spiteful," Sala said.

Ahmad embraced him and whispered, "Thank you."

For the next few days, Sala spent his time going back and forth between Watraan and the jungle. Ahmad's family had become part of his life.

As time passed, Ahmad's grandchildren grew accustomed to the millipedes, frogs, and forest rats. If a frog or lizard crawled onto their blanket, they no longer screamed. When a forest rat darted across Sarah's drawing book, Ega picked it up as if it were a stuffed toy.

***

"Do you really believe that Christian man will not report us to the Reds?" Anton asked one night.

"If he wanted to, he could have done it the first day," Ahmad said.

"But we can't trust him just like that." Anton did not live in Watraan or know Sala.

"He will never give us away. I know him well," Ahmad retorted.

A week later, Sala told Ahmed to return to the village with his family. A military post had been set up in Watraan. Few refugees found the courage to return, and Ahmad joined them. But Sala was going to Langgur. He wanted to volunteer.

***

Sala walked for hours. The smell of the forest was gone by the time he reached the gate to Langgur village. Just a short distance away a group of men wearing red bandanas, from teenagers to the elderly, blocked the gate. They stood in a row like the wooden boards used to break the waves, and carried long swords with tips touching the ground. They confronted a woman wearing a red jilbab and five young men.

"Please help me. I want to go to Langgur and find my sister," the woman pleaded. Her sister had settled in Langgur several years earlier after marrying a local young man. Sala walked up to the group.

"Pela, I'm from Watraan and seeking refuge here." He held out his hand in greeting.

Hearing the word "pela" triggered a switch in the men, bringing memories of their ancestors, the rock inscribed with blood, a blood toast drunk together. The men grasped Sala by the shoulder and nodded.

"Pela, where have you been? I've been looking for you. How is your mother? This upheaval has brought suffering to everyone."

Sala knew the voice well.

Max stepped forward from the group of men. He clapped Sala on the shoulder and hugged him. Max and Sala had gone to high school together in Tual.

Sala looked at the woman with the red jilbab. She had the face of his mother. The men with the red headbands were guarding the church in their village. It sheltered many refugees, Protestants and Muslims alike.

"Can this woman and I come in?"

An old man who appeared to be leading the group nodded.

The woman thanked Sala profusely. During their journey, she talked about her two sisters who were married to Protestant men. She hoped that at a time like this, they would help one another.

***

Outside the church was another group of men, who Sala joined in standing guard. They were quiet, alert, and appeared tense. Sala had wanted to volunteer, but now he wavered. He worried Langgur might suffer the same fate as Watraan. The thought occurred to leave Southeast Maluku. But how? He had no relatives to ask for help; neither did he know where his mother's relatives might be. His mother had never introduced them. His great-aunt had never seen him. His grandfather, La Kape, was only a visitor to Watraan. Martina had never told Sala who his great-aunt was. When La Kape and his wife Maria died, Maria's sister raised Martina. But Martina was not happy with them.

Nineteen years ago, Martina committed a transgression. She had become pregnant with Sala before she said her marital vows in church. Her whole family bore the shame. The family agreed that if she had a boy, he would not be allowed to carry the clan name. So when Martina's child was born, he was only given the one name: Sala. There was no family name since they had disowned Martina.

His mother dominated Sala's memories. His father was a stranger who had stopped on Kei Kecil to study the island's Damar flycatcher and the pied imperial pigeon. He had thought the two birds were still common on Kei.

He fell in love with Martina, who was then thirty-eight. The villagers said she would have been an old maid if not for that stranger. Her dark complexion and curly hair had drawn him to her. But before the priest could announce the wedding and Martina could dress up, the man had returned to his country.

Sala knew him from a sepia-tinted photograph. He wore a shirt with the top three buttons opened and a pair of jeans. He had a light beard. Every time his mother talked about the foreigner, she paused in her description. "I've forgotten if his hair was blond like butter or nutmeg or sand. What I do remember are his eyes, yes, his gray eyes," Martina said, her own eyes sparkling.

"His forehead wrinkled when he spoke Indonesian haltingly, but he always told me fluently, 'You know I love you, Tina.'

"Whenever he went into the jungle, he always came back with birds. He tied something to their legs. I never understood what he did. After a few days, he would return to the jungle and let the birds go. Is that strange?

"He said he was an orni… ornito… oh, orni something, I forget."

"Ornithologist, Mother," Sala said.

"Yes, that's what he said, ornithologist. Ah, your father would be proud to know he has such a clever son."

Martina was hard to stop once she started talking about the foreign man. She spoke about him unceasingly, the way a man might go on about a soccer game.

Her eyes shone like the stars just before the break of dawn. Her smile spread as she recalled the past. The memories never ceased, and she had her own way of bringing them back.

She had never blamed the foreigner. For her, it was fate, and fate sometimes had its own way of teaching people how to love, respect, and forgive.

The foreigner, whose name Martina never told Sala, had left for America without ever knowing she was pregnant. All she had known about his home was the name of the continent. That was what she told Sala.

For his part, Sala had no desire to find his father.

Chapter 5

Langgur, April 1999

Inside the cramped and stuffy church, the smell of burning mosquito coils hung heavy in the air. Namira sank into her own stillness. The song *"Puing"* by Iwan Fals on the guard's radio in front of the church made her sad.

Every time she drew a breath, she heard sniffles from her congested nose. Where were her parents? Why had no one come looking for her? Her sniffles turned to sobs that grew louder. In the still of the night, Namira only heard her own crying and the breathing of the other sleeping refugees. She thought about her father and mother. The only clothes she had were the ones she wore: a faded purple top and a knee-length red skirt. In her escape through the jungle, the strap of one sandal had broken. She prayed with all her heart to see her parents again.

A cold wind blew outside the church and seeped through the gap around the window above her head. The rustle of bamboo leaves turned into a strange whistling. The men standing guard outside did not speak. Their stomachs rumbled from hunger but they did not think about dinner. News came from Tual and the southern islands, increasing everyone's anxiety. The unrest brought only hunger and fear.

Namira hugged her knees and leaned against the church wall with peeling paint. She looked at the glass of water; she had only taken one sip. A packet of cookies with a picture of creamy peanut butter did nothing to whet her appetite.

The woman next to her had been asleep for the past hour. Her daughter, about five years old, rested in the crook of her plump arm. A volunteer had lit a mosquito coil with the picture of an owl on its package in the center of the church. It burned down to a small ring. Namira tried to stifle her crying when a man came into the church to fetch a box of bottled water and take it outside.

Only women and children were inside the church. All the men stood guard outside. Protecting the women was a tradition that ran through the veins of Kei men. It was a teaching from the ancestors.

Namira stood and looked around. Above her head was a window with murky glass. She put her face to it until she almost kissed the pane. The crescent moon shed a pale light. Sheaves of dried palm fronds were scattered by the side of the church and looked like sleeping monitor lizards. The brush that needed to be cleared formed a creepy silhouette.

She thought of her mother, Samrina. Before Namira left to fetch the sago her father had crushed, her mother had gone out. Samrina headed for Ngursoin to deliver the curtains a church official had asked her to sew. Namira had folded the curtains before putting it into a blue plastic bag with a picture of Mickey Mouse. The day before, her mother had worked on them until late at night. Namira had asked her several times to rest, but Samrina told her to go to sleep and not wait up. "I need to finish this curtain first. If the conflict reaches our village, I won't be able to take these curtains to Ngursoin. A promise is a promise. The customer has to be served on time and with all our heart," Samrina said. While the rest of Elaar waited anxiously for news of the spreading conflict, she thought about her customer in another village.

"In that case I'll stay with you."

Samrina stopped rocking the pedal of her sewing machine. She got up from her seat and hugged Namira. Holding her only daughter tight, her tears fell onto Namira's hair. Samrina was truly worried that night. Two days earlier she had gone to the market, where people talked about a woman in Ambon who had the muzzle of an M-16 rifle shoved into her face by a soldier.

"It's pointless trusting the authorities. They are only here to stir up more trouble. A relative told me they are on the side of the Reds. The authorities and the Reds are going after the Whites. In Ambon the authorities are allowing the attacks."

Samrina gently chided a woman who was talking loudly. "Don't talk like that. It's best to stay quiet. Things are the same here. One misspoken word can lead to a big fight."

"What do you know? You sit at home and sew. Many of our people are being killed. In January during the *Idul Fitri* worship, the Reds attacked before Muslims had a chance to forgive one another. You don't know what it is like to celebrate Idul Fitri in the shadow of death."

The woman cried and beat her chest as she spoke. Samrina left the market without buying anything.

***

Namira dried her eyes with the tail of her blouse. She was about to lie down when a man started waking the sleeping women and children.

"Get up. We have just heard on the radio that Tual, Wab, Ohoibadar, and Elaar are on fire. The women and children must go to Langgur, where it is still safe."

So, this was what it felt like to flee from one village to another, a refugee in one's home. Everyone rose at once. The children, fast asleep a moment before, woke up startled and cried. Namira held a two-year-old child while her mother busily packed for the journey.

The woman put a blanket and a bottle of eucalyptus oil into a baby bag. "What is your name?"

"Namira."

"I'm Esme Labetubun, but just call me Esme. The only things I brought when we fled were for my child and a few jewels for safekeeping. I have not heard from my husband.

He left for Ambon four months ago to take care of our lobster business. I hope he is far from the conflict."

"I hope you see him again."

"Thank you. Where are your parents?"

"I lost them."

"What village are you from?"

"Elaar."

"I'm from Dobo, in the Aru islands."

Esme took the child from Namira and pulled the girl close to her. They shared the same problem; both had lost track of their loved ones. Esme stroked Namira's head and channeled her strength to the young girl.

Namira looked at Esme. The woman was determined. Talking with her made Namira feel she was no longer alone.

Two men named Sat and Bituk escorted the women to the beach. The white sand was cold beneath their feet. A motorboat sent by the Ohoinol village chief waited for them.

Under the light of a waning moon, the women filed into the boat. Namira looked at the sky. A star twinkled below the crescent moon. It seemed to move closer. Namira's mother once told her a star beneath the crescent moon meant there would be death. A star above a full moon meant the wedding season had begun.

When Namira was nine, she and her mother had waited for her father to return from the sea. Awash in the light of the full moon, Namira sang cheerfully:

> *The moon under an umbrella, the turtle*
> *lays its eggs*

The lady from Ambon comes to the marriage office
Stay happily married, never fight
If you fight, it is best you seek a divorce.

Samrina laughed at her daughter's singing. "It would be better if you sang a Kei song. Our language was used to give praise, sing church songs, and recite the Lord's Prayer. Now everyone uses the national language. Kei is only used in everyday conversation. Few kids these days can speak Kei fluently."

The light of the moon turned the surface of the sea into ripples of gold, like fish scales catching the sunlight. In the distance, the fishermen and their boats looked like black rocks bobbing on the gold-ringed water.

In Namira's eyes, her mother was an intriguing woman. She was a seamstress, a renowned tifa player from Elaar, and an herbal healer. Samrina's knowledge about leaves, twigs, and roots that could be used for medicine was boundless. She was like a cross between a zoologist and a documentary filmmaker.

Namira loved her mother. Until she was seventeen, Namira could only fall asleep by having her mother tell a bedtime story. One night Samrina told her the story of an old woman who brought water to her barren village. Another night she told her about "Lateo and the Dolphin Princess." And the night following, she had yet a different tale: "Te Idar" or "Princess Kayani and the Spy." These stories were told for decades, yet they still had the power to put Namira to sleep.

***

The night was cold as the motorboat carrying the refugees headed around the coast for Langgur. Crashing waves wrapped the hull of the boat like the folds of a funeral shroud. Her teeth chattering, Namira clamped her knees together.

Esme unfurled a sarong with a hand-painted picture of a stork. The picture reminded Namira of the large basin at home. It had a picture of a white stork pecking at the fish surrounding him. After returning from sea, her father would empty his fishing basket into the basin, as though offering the fish to the stork.

Namira felt comfortable near Esme. She was a talkative woman. She told Namira how she had been to Langgur several times. Her husband sold lobsters and pearls. Every new moon he would ask Esme to visit the churches on the other islands, including Langgur, to distribute alms. Most of the people from Dobo had a lot of money. In Southeast Maluku, Dobo was known as "The Dollar."

Namira suspected Esme to be very wealthy. A popular saying among the people of Southeast Maluku was, "If you want to be rich, live in Dobo; if you want to be a politician and stick to tradition, move to Tual; if you want to be pious and devout, stay in Saumlaki; and if you want to be steadfast, live in Tepa or Kisar." Tepa and Kisar were remote islands at the southeastern end of the archipelago, close to

East Timor. The people of Southeast Maluku considered them places of exile.

"My husband often travels around the islands. He has been to Saumlaki and Tamadan. He visits churches to share his fortune. Ah, I really miss him."

"My mother said that people who like to share are always rich in their hearts. I miss my mother," Namira said with a sob.

"Your mother must be a very good person. If the safety of our village is restored and my house is still standing, I want you to come and stay with me. I'll cook lobster for you."

Namira smiled and nodded. She was happy Esme shared her good cheer.

***

The motorboat moored off the coast near Langgur. In the distance could be seen silhouettes of people. Five men guarded them like soldiers at a border crossing. The radio had announced that refugees were coming to Langgur.

They were divided into two groups, one to be sheltered in the church, and the other at the home of Father Gerardus. The refugees trusted their fate to God. Esme went to the pastor's house, while Namira found herself assigned to the church.

Esme hugged Namira. She took off her gold chain with a crucifix pendant. Namira was shocked at the sight and instinctively stepped back. Esme understood the expression on the Muslim girl's face.

She pressed the chain and pendant into Namira's palm. "Take this. If you need money, you can sell it."

"But—"

"The fighting in Kei has nothing to do with Islam or Christianity. God and religion never betray their believers. Only mankind betrays God and religion.

"Take this," she repeated. "It's all I can give you. Don't look down on the cross. Regard it as gold. Who knows, if you need anything, you can always sell it."

Namira hugged Esme tightly. In the middle of conflict, there was still goodness. Esme showed concern about her fate. Namira waved as Esme walked to Father Gerardus's house before she followed two of the guards to the village church.

They walked along a footpath behind a row of houses, past the city hall where a group of people talked in the light of a hurricane lantern, and squeezed between the houses, ducking under the branches of *bael* trees. The large and round green fruit hung like heads in the darkness.

"Ouch, my foot!" Namira screamed.

"Miss, are you alright?" The wavy-haired young guard told his friend to shine his flashlight at Namira's foot. Blood poured from the sole.

"Let me take out this shard of glass, otherwise your foot will get infected." He took off his shirt and rolled it up tightly. He asked Namira to bite down on the rolled-up shirt, so her screams would be muffled and not scare the others. In the current unrest, a scream easily sparked fear and prejudice against strangers.

Namira hobbled behind the young man who had pulled the piece of broken bottle from her foot. "What is your name?"

"Sala. I have no clan name. And you?"

"Namira." She turned to the man beside Sala as he shined his flashlight on the ground ahead.

"Max."

***

The backyard of the church was transformed into a soup kitchen, where women from a humanitarian volunteer team cooked meals for the refugees. Three large rocks were arranged to form a triangle. On top, a large pot spewed out steam. Namira joined in the cooking. There was no point in feeling sad. The tears she shed every night did not make her mother and father come looking for her. The brown-eyed girl wiped down the long table with a rag and lined up dishes of food for the refugees.

Namira was chopping bitter melons when Sala came in carrying a string of grouper and basket of clams.

"We went fishing. The women who are nursing have only been eating instant noodles."

Sala placed the fish in a basin on the table in front of Namira. She was surprised to hear his explanation. It was rare for a man his age to be concerned about the wellbeing of nursing mothers.

"How is your foot?" he asked.

"It's much better."

Sala left without saying anything else.

Namira sprinkled salt on the slices of bitter melon in an aluminum pan. The salt helped lessen the bitterness of the vegetable. While she cooked with the other women, four men stepped out of the church's back door. One of them held a motionless baby wrapped in a cloth.

"What is going on?" a volunteer asked.

"The baby died."

Behind the men, the mother covered her face with her hands and wept. The men dug a hole some distance from the cooking fire and buried the baby. The child had died from vomiting and diarrhea.

Namira thought of Esme and her baby. She prayed in her heart that mother and child would always be healthy.

At seven that night, the women carried platters of yams, vegetables, and fish stew. The men took turns eating and standing guard. Sala helped Namira take the dirty plates to the well in the back. He drew water for Namira and helped wash the plates.

"You look gloomy. What's the matter?"

"A baby died earlier this afternoon." Namira rinsed off the soapsuds clinging to the plates. When she was little, she had enjoyed helping her mother wash dishes because she was allowed to play with the soapsuds to her heart's content. She would gather the foam from the sink and put it into an empty soap dish, and then scooped up the bubbles with a small coil and blew them all over the kitchen. She had loved seeing the bubbles turn into rainbows when hit by sunlight.

When she was done with the dishes, Namira found a seat beneath the *ketapang* tree that fanned over the churchyard. She had been indoors for too long and needed fresh air. In the distant sky, she saw only the twinkle of stars. Clouds blocked the moon. A breeze scattered leaves around her.

Something cool pressed against the sole of her foot. Sala was bandaging her wound with a piece of torn cloth.

"Don't be disgusted. I chewed the *antanan* leaves first. Your foot will heal quickly. Bandage it like this so dirt stays out of the wound."

"You scared me. Next time you want to help someone, at least ask for permission."

Namira shivered, annoyed.

"I'm sorry. What are you doing here?"

"I was thinking."

"What about?"

"This conflict must end soon. I miss my parents and my best friend in Evu. We used to dance together until the war separated us. Mery is Catholic and I'm Muslim."

"I'm Protestant," Sala said, straight-faced. "The conflict doesn't have to divide us. We are all one. We have one set of ancestors and were born in the same place, the island of Kei."

Namira was quiet. Sala dropped next to her, resting his hands behind him. Neither of them spoke.

A few moments later, Sala said. "One day, the mosque in my village was hit by a strong gust of wind and the roof was damaged. Our church congregation helped repair the mosque. I was there too. The imam said, 'It is not because we live in the same village or have different faiths that you have helped us repair our mosque. What happened today is that we are continuing what our ancestors did before us. This mosque belongs to all of us, so let us use it as a place of worship according to our respective beliefs.'

"I liked seeing you in the kitchen earlier, helping to cook for the refugees. You don't care whether they are Muslim, Protestant, or Catholic. You are motivated by a sense of humanity. And that is exactly what moved our ancestors."

The wave of violence sweeping across the islands was the second disaster in recent years, the first being a yearlong drought blamed on the El Niño heat wave that lasted from 1997 to 1998.

During that time, the earth dried up and cracked. The wind dried the skin and lips. All that was left in the wells was mud. The roads were dusty, and the small islands throughout Kei were beset by food shortages. Many men were forced to leave their villages and go to Papua to make a living. Only women and children stayed behind. But the Kei women had always been known for their strength. They worked the dry fields, gathered clams, and went out to sea for fish. The extraordinary resilient women of Kei overcame the heat wave that had turned the forests of Sumatra and Borneo into seas of fire.

"I would like to tell you a story. Are you interested?" Sala asked.

Namira nodded. Since he had pulled the shard from her foot, she felt she had made a new friend. Sala had the same goodness as Mery.

"Two nights ago, after I brought you and the other refugees here, I joined a meeting of the tribal elders in the city hall. They had talked about reconciliation. The *Larwul Ngabal* is the only way to end the war."

Larwul Ngabal was the traditional law of the Kei. When it was read, people were struck dumb and cried. The history of terrible violence between two villages necessitated this law. Punishment for those who violated the Larwul Ngabal was severe. The law had prevailed for four centuries.

Namira looked at Sala. He was an unusual man. His knowledge was rare, and his views on life were very traditional.

Sala told the story he had wanted to share since he first saw the Muslim girl with the volunteers.

He had found a book left behind by his grandmother, Maria, inside an ironwood chest, and had carefully blown away the yellow beads left by bookworms on some of the pages. After spending three nights reading it, he donated the book to the public library in Tual. The book explained the Larwul Ngabal, how it was born from the thought and conscience of a woman called Dit Sak Mas.

"One day a wandering woman named Dit Sak Mas traveled by water buffalo from Woma Rer on the west coast of Kei Kecil to Danar in the southeast," Sala began.

"Do all folk tales start with 'one day'?" Namira chuckled, teasing him.

He laughed. "Do you want me to continue or not?"

"Of course. I was just joking. Sorry."

"She went on this journey to find a man worthy of being her life companion. In the middle of the journey, two men accosted Dit Sak Mas and robbed her. They took all her supplies. However, she did not despair. She went back to Woma Rer and gathered more supplies.

"While wondering how to avoid being robbed again, Dit Sak Mas had a revelation. She tied a yellow palm frond to her food containers and set off on her journey again.

"Throughout the journey, no one seeing the yellow palm fronds dared to rob her. The palm fronds later became known as *hawear*—a sacred sign that forbids anyone from taking what rightfully belongs to another person. Over time, it became a tradition to use hawear to protect things, including nature and the environment. It is from this story that the Tutup Sasi Laut ceremony was conceived."

Namira was impressed by Sala's knowledge. "I like that story," she said.

Sala looked closely at her face to read her sincerity, but it was in vain; the fading light made it impossible to see her eyes clearly.

His voice quavered. "I have lots of stories from the past, if you want to meet here again tomorrow night."

Namira nodded and rose, blushing. Dried ketapang leaves crackled beneath her feet as she walked away, leaving Sala in disbelief at his asking a girl for a date. Since his schooldays in Tual, he had been known for being cold toward girls. He was different from his friend Max, who was always changing dance partners.

***

The days trudged by during the unrest. Every village was paralyzed. The markets, kiosks, clinics, power plants, and schools—nothing was open. Meanwhile in Jakarta, legislators and government officials talked about peace inside air-conditioned rooms.

The grief of the refugees gave Sala the idea of convincing Max to give them a musical performance twice a week. "I hate talking about peace inside a room. It doesn't change what is happening outside," said Sala. "There are many things we can do. You can sing, Max, and I can play the guitar. We'll give the refugees a little entertainment."

When they were at school in Tual, Max and Sala were members of their church's youth music group. They performed every time there was a service for the young people of the congregation. Max sang hymns while Sala played guitar. Now they performed for the refugees on Tuesday and Saturday nights.

On this particular Tuesday, the refugees left their tents and gathered in front of the Langgur church to listen to Max's singing. There were songs by Iwan Fals, the Kla Project, Arwana, and Java Jive. Max launched into a rendition of "*Terlalu Manis*" by Slank:

> *I take my guitar and begin playing*
> *Old songs that we can sing*
> *Only memories are in my head*
> *The day changes, the wind keeps blowing*
> *The weather changes, the leaves keep*
>   *growing.*

Amid the other refugees, Namira sat dazzled as Sala played his guitar to the Slank song that Max sang a second time. His voice made some of the volunteers shed tears when he slipped into the next song.

I want peace, I want calm.
I want peace, I want calm.

***

The unrest became more unnerving. Food aid for the refugees only came from foreign donors and the government outside Maluku, and most of what they received was various brands of instant noodles, and bread gone stale because transport to the islands was difficult.

Sala collected Daud, Hans, and two refugees named Ahmad and Yusuf, and went to meet the Langgur village chief to ask permission to use his boat to go fishing. The rest of the refugees and residents stayed behind, keeping the village safe.

Every day before dawn, Namira went to see off Sala and waited for him to return in the afternoon. Since Namira had stepped on the glass, Sala treated her like a little sister. When she had an upset stomach one night after eating too many clams, she woke him up and he took her to the beach. He stayed with her as she emptied her bowels, sitting next to her as she squatted even though he had to gasp for air. When she needed to urinate in the middle of the night, she would go to his tent, find his sleeping body, and tug on his toe. He would wake up immediately and go with her.

One afternoon Namira had a headache and vomited after inadvertently eating some of the stale bread. Sala panicked and carried her to the health clinic. He waited while she was treated and turned into one of those nagging old women, constantly reminding Namira to take her medicine. He checked on her in her tent before going to sleep.

Since Sala and Namira were often seen together, no other man dared flirt with her. The members of the refugee camp pretty much agreed that Namira was Sala's girlfriend.

Sala took her for walks. He promised Namira that once the conflict was over, he would take her to Ternate and the Kalamata Fort to see the cannons. He also promised to take her to Lake Laguna and Mount Daab. On the mountain, they could look for imperial pigeons and cockatoos. He knew she loved animals. Namira had dreams of being an ornithologist. It was a strange coincidence, a kind of serendipity. His mother, Martina, had told him that his own father was an ornithologist.

Namira was radiant on the afternoon Sala invited her to Daud's house to meet Bun Lai, a parrot. The bird was very clever and could say good evening, *assalamu alaikum*, shalom, honey, pretty lady, and help.

When they arrived at the small house with its bamboo walls, Bun Lai got up and fluffed his tail, shouting, "Pretty lady! Pretty lady!" Namira laughed. Daud told Bun Lai to say "assalamu alaikum" to greet Namira, and the sweet creature with the shiny green feathers and red head said the phrase twice.

Daud had found Bun Lai in the middle of the sea, perched on a piece of wood studded with barnacles. Bun Lai could not fly because his previous owner, a crewmember on the *Long Ki*, had clipped his wings. The owner had failed to keep an eye on his bird, and one day the parrot walked on the deck, only to be swept overboard by a gust of wind.

When Daud was at sea, he saw the shivering parrot perched on a piece of driftwood. He swam out, retrieved the parrot, and brought it back to his boat. The parrot became his.

***

Namira woke earlier than usual. The sky was still a thick blue and the earth not yet lit up. In the east, the morning star shimmered perfectly. That day Sala planned to leave Langgur as a volunteer truck driver and deliver donations of rice to Ngilngof, one of the villages west of Langgur. He had promised to look for firewood on his return, since the supplies for the soup kitchen were running low.

"How long will you be in Ngilngof?"

"Three days."

"*Three days?*"

"If the road is safe, maybe only two."

"That's a long time," Namira sighed.

"The rice can help many people. Pout like that and you'll end up looking like Aunt Kribo in camp three."

"Stop teasing me. Go and bring back a lot of firewood." Namira turned away. She did not want Sala to see her eyes misting over. The truth was, she was sick with worry. In the conflict, not a single road between the villages was safe. Namira prayed and banished from her mind every image of Sala's truck rolling over, or getting a flat tire, or being accosted by rioters, or extorted.

The crunch of the truck tires on the gravel road and smell of exhaust made Namira lonely. She wondered about her feelings for Sala.

In the rearview mirror, Sala saw Namira stand by the side of the road. The figure grew smaller the further he went until she disappeared from view. He had barely left, but already missed her.

Chapter 6

Unrest in the country's spice-growing belt began seven months after President Suharto resigned in May 1998, when the streets of Jakarta were taken over by protesters and Scorpions—the black English-made tanks whose sale had sparked controversy in London. The tanks were used to disperse the student protesters on the streets demanding President Suharto to step down. They chanted, "Suharto is Hitler," and carried banners with messages parodying the song "My Heart Will Go On" from the film, *Titanic*, to read "My Harto Will Go On To Hell."

Village elders said, "Don't do that to Pak Harto. This country would be in ruins if not for a strong and dignified leader like him."

Suharto's New Order ended like a thriller movie on a flat note. Rumors spread through the churches in Maluku that Suharto had sent agents to incite tension between people of different religions. It was barely credible, since Suharto had already resigned. However, public van drivers, clove growers, and pearl farmers in Ambon believed it.

Several months after Suharto's downfall, violence broke out in Ambon. Few people in Maluku believed it would spread to the furthest reaches of the Kei islands. The inhabitants were known for their strong embrace of tradition. Everyone in Maluku knew the Kei people were strong believers in the law of Larwul Ngabal. They had worn the armor of the law for four centuries, since the time of wars between tribes, and withstood the arrival of the major religions. Larwul Ngabal had survived the Dutch colonization and the birth of the centralized New Order. The Kei men watching the violence on the television set at Sipora's noodle stall said the conflict would never reach Southeast Maluku.

"We have to make sure it doesn't spread to here," said Hutman, a worker on a sago farm.

"Everyone has sworn the traditional oath. There's no way the conflict will reach us," said Saha, a fisherman. For half an hour, the sago worker and fisherman argued about whether the conflict would reach Kei.

The conversation on that day in February was just the idle chatter of customers who enjoyed Sipora's fiery hot noodle soup that was famous for burning the tongue. However, the unrest was like a flame with the power to spread anywhere, consuming everything in its path.

***

In the town of Tual, capital of the Southeast Maluku province, the Larwul Ngabal was inscribed on a two-meter high wall that stood at the intersection of the main streets. No one suspected the unrest would come to Kei. The only outcome of the conflict that Sala did not regret was meeting Namira. Violence had thrown communities into the past, the mysticism of their ancestors and fear of enmity. But it had also given birth to a mysterious love in the refugee camp, one that crossed religious lines and blossomed in the middle of war.

The full moon shone bright as Sala and Namira found each other again beneath the ketapang tree. They sat on the dried leaves. Earlier in the day, children from the refugee camp had picked the fallen fruits. The seeds tasted like peanuts. Samrina once told Namira the leaves could cure leprosy and scabies.

Sometimes Max joked about the young couple. He said Namira and Sala were like the nightjar and the fern. They needed each other, protected each other, and were inseparable. Namira was made for the young man's lonely soul, and Sala was made to be Namira's older brother in a time of conflict.

That night, Namira rambled about her pet goat, Famur, her unfulfilled desire to raise sheep, her mother's sewing machine that often refused to work, and her best friend Mery; Sala listened to her intently. Only for a fleeting moment did his thoughts wander to the porcelain tea set he had buried behind his house. Namira stopped when a loud conversation started behind them.

Not far from where they sat, two members of the humanitarian volunteer corps talked about President Suharto. Namira and Sala listened in.

"Do you like Suharto?"

"Why do we have to talk about him?"

"Nothing wrong with talking about him. Besides, the New Order is gone."

"It only just happened," said the female volunteer.

"I always thought the conflict in Maluku was a payback for Suharto's 'economic miracle.' Our cultures, customs, and traditions have been looted by American corporations and the like," the male volunteer said.

"What do you mean?"

"The conflict is part of the effort to safeguard the resources American corporations have been after. Before Suharto stepped down, he was pressured by the International Monetary Fund to stop all fuel and food subsidies. That kind of policy was clearly meant to benefit the rich and result in starvation, violence in the regions, and disease.

"Rice is the main cause. When we did not have to rely on Jakarta for everything, and the people of Kei grew up healthy. We were rarely ill even though we only ate cassava and sago." The man paused to take a deep breath that expressed his deep frustration with the condition of the country.

"Before he resigned, people were afraid of talking about Suharto or the Banyan Tree Party. Village chiefs prohibited their people from saying anything bad about Suharto. They warned the villagers, 'You will go to jail, or get kidnapped in the dead of night, or fired as a civil servant. Or most scary, used as bait for sharks or food for crocodiles.'"

The volunteer continued with passion: "I didn't like Suharto, or his government. Suharto is most responsible for weakening the traditional customs throughout the country. He was the one who decided to replace the traditional chiefs with salaried village chiefs. He imposed a uniform administrative structure on all 67,000 villages in the country, so that traditional laws slowly became neutered and died. He also set up the Village Consultative Board and the Village Community Resilience Board. Just hearing those names makes me sick to my stomach."

"Don't say that. As bad as anyone is, they still have some goodness. I actually preferred him to Sukarno. Suharto did not drink. He remained faithful to his wife. Unlike officials these days, he rarely went abroad. Suharto was a president who was a farmer," the woman said calmly. She spoke about Suharto as though she was a friend of his children.

"Why do you talk about Suharto, Suharto, Suharto the whole time? I'm tired of it. I won't listen to any more of your babbling," the woman went on in a harsh voice. She had expected a different, sweeter conversation. She got up and left in a huff.

"Is it my turn to talk?" Namira asked with a giggle. "Tell me, am I the first woman you have fallen for?"

"Hmm, there was another woman I liked before you."

"Where is she now?"

"I don't know."

"Come on, tell me. Quit trying to be mysterious. It doesn't suit you," she goaded him.

Sala looked at the sky as though it held his childhood, when he watched his mother forge machetes under the full moon. He had loved seeing the sparks fly from the blades as the hammer struck. The sparks looked like the fireworks on New Year's Eve.

The metal shop held many memories of him and his mother. He had seen the full moon clearly from the roofless shed. In the center of the sphere, an old man bent over a fishing net. Sala had asked his mother about it, and Martina said the old man was mending his trawl net.

"Why hasn't he finished after all these years, Mama?" he persisted.

"Every time the net is almost ready, a group of rats comes and nibbles at the stiches," Martina said, guffawing.

When he was in the fifth grade, he learned his mother had made up the story.

Namira's face lit by the full moon was beautiful and dramatic. Sala sometimes imagined that her face was a dandelion—sweet, innocent, and simple. He remembered an anecdote from his youth. "When I was seven years old I liked one of my classmates. I stole a pencil and sharpener from a store near my school just so I could give her a gift. I waited for her to pass and I gave her the stolen pencil and sharpener."

Namira laughed freely. She found the story genuinely entertaining.

Ever since he knew Namira, Sala had laughed again. Ever since she met Sala, Namira had lost her gloomy expression.

Sala held her hand, lacing his fingers with hers. "I love you," he said in a low voice. Namira gasped. It felt as if they were the only people.

***

Namira and Sala wiped down the floor and the seats after the Saturday night performance for the congregation the next day.

On Sunday morning, some of the refugees dressed up. They carried bibles as they entered the church. Namira watched them, their faces calm as they arrived to worship their God. She remembered when her father used to lead the *salat* prayers.

Sala stepped from the tent next to hers, wearing a black shirt and faded jeans. Joining the churchgoers, he looked at Namira and smiled. Only the Muslim refugees were left in the tent. It was quiet. Those not praying showed their respect for those who were.

Namira walked behind the tent to the window at the side of the church. She wanted to see how Sala prayed. She looked at the people inside. The priest gave a sermon on a theme of peace. He told the congregation not to get involved in any fighting and recited a verse from the Bible: "'If I speak in the tongues of men or of angels, but do not have love, I am only a resounding gong or a clanging cymbal.' This teaches us that love supersedes everything. It

is love that can ease violence in turbulent times like these,"
the priest said in a loud voice. After that, everyone sang.

Namira caught a glimpse of Sala. When she looked at
him hard enough, he resembled the actor James Franco in
the movie, *Tristan + Isolde.* Inside the church, he appeared
to be singing. Namira moved from the window. She went
back to the tent and found the female volunteer who had
the argument the previous night, handing out diarrhea
medicine and rubbing oil.

"Is anyone sick?" Namira asked.

"Not in this camp, but the villages of Ngadi and Dulla
on the north coast have many children with diarrhea
and vomiting. Two infants died over there yesterday," the
volunteer said quietly. The news had saddened her.

"Can I help?"

The volunteer turned. "Take these medicines. Distribute
them in the other tents. Tell them to keep them just in case."

Namira picked up a box and visited each tent.

Sala left the church at the end of the service to follow
her. He truly loved the girl.

Later that night he took Namira to the beach and told
her about the golden teardrops of Kei women. The men
of Kei were taught to respect their women. The Larwul
Ngabal said that a Kei woman's tears were like gold—they
must not be spilled in vain. True Kei men only went to war
to defend their women's honor.

The new moon cast a curving arc of yellow light over
the water. As Namira listened to Sala, she leaned her head
against his shoulder.

***

The next day held a happy surprise for Namira.

Mery appeared in front of her tent with outstretched arms. She looked sad, but tried to smile. The two girls hugged. Mery had tried hard to find out what had happened to Namira. She brought clothes and medicines, as well as a bag of her mother's *bagea* cakes. They hugged and cried.

Sala watched from a distance. He wanted to give Namira a chance to catch up with her friend.

When Mery asked Uncle Orlando to let her remain at the camp, he said, "You can't stay, Mery." But she was stubborn and refused to leave. Orlando shook his head, and then left the girls to join the other men.

"Ra, I have two pieces of news for you. The first is that I really miss my best friend. The second is…" Mery could not continue.

"And the second piece?" Namira suddenly had a bad feeling. Her heart beat faster.

Mery took Namira's arm and led her from the tent. They took a seat on the church steps.

Sorrow came in the wake of the happiness Mery had brought with her. The body of Namira's father had been found washed up on the Banda Eli Beach, far from home. As for her mother, Mery had done the best she could but there was no trace of her.

Namira was dumbstruck. Blood drained from her face and her joints felt weak. The vision of a bleak future appeared before her.

Mery hugged her friend, trying to support to Namira.

That night they slept side by side in silence. There was none of the chatter that usually went on before they went to sleep, gossiping about the meanest teachers in their school while listening to Nike Ardila and Poppy Mercury songs.

Mery understood. Their lives had changed.

The next day at sunset, Namira said goodbye to Mery on the beach before she headed back to her village. They hugged again. "You still love me even though I'm a Muslim?" Namira's eyes were puffy.

"Don't talk like that, Ra. There are no Muslims or Christians. We know this is not a religious war, it's a political fight incited by people who have no qualms about exploiting religious differences. They want to take away our natural resources. We can't be like the Dutch, who used religion as a political tool to rule Maluku in the past." Mery panted like a demonstrator.

It was the first time Namira saw her friend so serious. "When can we meet again?" she asked.

"As soon as possible, Ra, once our village is safe. I already asked Mama to have you come to Evu. She said that you should stay here for now. An anonymous letter circulated in Evu, saying that any Catholic found sheltering a Muslim will be beaten."

Mery hugged Namira again. She whispered, "Eat the cakes. It was the first chance Mama had to go to the kitchen. Mama and Papa are thinking of you. We pray that the conflict will be over soon."

Uncle Orlando was moved at seeing the friendship between the two girls.

He pushed the longboat from the beach and Namira burst into sobs. Sitting on the beach, she clutched a handful of sand, brought her hands to her face, and howled. The wound in her heart was unbearably painful. She buried her face in her hands.

Sala went up to Namira and placed his hand on her shoulder. She was at her most vulnerable. He took her to Max's house.

They walked past plasterboard houses and rows of coconut trees. Two children played with a dog in the front yard of Max's home. Next door, a man hung out his fishing net to dry. Langgur was still peaceful.

Max invited Namira to stay at his house while his parents, both church officials, traveled the islands off the west coast of Kei Kecil with food and medicine. The room Max showed her was covered with pictures of Jesus, the Virgin Mary, and Mother Theresa in wood frames. A Christmas tree from the previous year stood in the corner.

Sala led Namira into the bathroom. "Take a bath and you'll feel better. My mother used to take a bath whenever she felt sad." He asked her to bend over and poured water over her head. Sala washed her hair with a shampoo that smelled of honey and lime. He left her to rinse off the suds and waited outside the bathroom.

Once she had dressed, Sala led her to a bed with a java cotton mattress covered in yellow sheets. He tucked her in and was about to leave when she started to sob.

Sala sat on the edge of the bed and wiped Namira's tears with his finger. His eyes were red as he held back his own grief. He always felt the same sadness that engulfed Namira.

"Have you ever cried during this whole conflict?" Namira suddenly asked.

Sala nodded.

"Tell me."

"I'll tell you later. Rest now."

"But don't leave." Namira tried to keep her eyes closed. "Tell me. I'll listen with my eyes closed."

Sala began, "I had gone to sell knives in Mun Kahar. Before I left, my mother told me to return quickly."

He fell silent and looked up at the ceiling. He could not bear to continue his story.

"And then?"

After a while, Sala resumed. "I found her body when I came home. I didn't have the chance to ask for her forgiveness." He bowed his head as he spoke about the source of his pain buried deep inside.

He had always thought that sharing sadness was foolish. Everyone had the same story. Besides, he was a man. His mother had often told him that men were not allowed to cry. A man must bear his sadness alone.

Namira was surprised as guilt washed over her. She sat up and took Sala in her arms. "I hope your mother is in heaven," she whispered.

"And your father too."

After a short silence, Sala said, "I want to promise you something: I'll protect you. You are the only one I love now."

Namira let go of Sala. The look in her eyes said she understood, but still seemed offended.

"What's wrong?" he asked.

"I don't need protection," she said.

"Are you angry with me?"

"I don't like that kind of talk."

"I'm sorry." Sala pulled Namira into his arms. "I'm sorry if you didn't like what I said. I just don't want to lose another person I love."

Namira remained silent, ashamed of her childish behavior.

"I'm sorry, okay? Are you still angry?"

Namira shook her head. "You're the only one I have."

Their bodies pressed close together. Sala's heart beat so loud that Namira could hear it. He felt the blood rushing to his head. The room filled with a deep silence. The heat from their bodies could have melted ice. Love and fear mingled to create a strange sensation while they experienced an ancient pleasure.

Namira shut her eyes tighter. Tears trickled from the corners of her eyes. The scent of Sala's perspiration and the weathered wood seeped into her senses.

The two of them fell asleep in each other's arms, entwined like a pair of swans.

Sala was first to wake. He looked at Namira's face, her eyes still closed. The sight sparked in him an awareness of love, as well as penitence. When Namira opened her eyes, Sala stroked her cheek.

"I want to marry you," Sala blurted.

Namira looked at his honey-brown eyes and strong jaw. In his eyes, she could not find any doubt, only determination and love.

"I'll marry you. Let me marry you," Sala repeated and spoke about all kinds of things. Would the wedding be in a church or a mosque? By an imam or a priest? He talked about witnesses, the porcelain tea set as a dowry, and the marriage certificate. About kebayas and babies and a house. About peace and the metal workshop he planned to revive, and having breakfast together.

Chapter 7

Evu, April 1999

Stillness crept over Mery during the boat trip. The sight of seagulls, a pod of dolphins, and the ever-changing clouds, no longer had the power to bring her a smile. The conflict had silenced everyone's laughter and cheer.

War took everything from everyone. Since the first fights broke out between youths from Tual and Taar, an area on the southern edge of Tual, the conflict had spread quickly, crossing the sea to the island of Kei Besar and back again to Kei Kecil.

On Kei Besar, the first hostilities were between the villages of Weduar Fer and Larat, before spreading across the water to Watraan, Elaar, Langgur—moving north and south, then to the islands off the south, west, and north coasts.

Mery watched as six dolphins surfaced. Those wonderful animals played and rubbed against each other, and protected and helped each other when danger approached. Kei used to be like that, people helping one another when threats loomed at the village gate.

Mery still felt Namira's sadness. Her father would have to be buried in Banda Eli, a village near the northeast coast of Kei Besar. Mery did not have the heart to tell Namira that the corpse was bloated when they found it, the skin peeling away, and parts of the flesh likely eaten by fish. Her father had been a tough seafarer, and he met his death at sea. He was from Banda Eli. Mery remembered that Namira's grandfather was also from there. She murmured, "Uncle Mohammad returns to the land of his ancestors."

As far back as Mery could remember, Namira's father always came home from the sea with the biggest mackerel. Mery and Namira would fight over the roe and fry it. Once he brought back reef fish, still twitching, and let Mery choose which ones to grill. "This is heaven, Mery. In big cities you will never find fish that died in the pot or on the grill."

"Over there the fish die a thousand times before they are sold," Namira joked. She and her father gathered dried coconut husks and piled them into a mound in the backyard. They lit the mound and grilled the fish on the embers, basting them with oil and lime juice. The aroma made Mery's stomach growl long before it was lunchtime.

When Mery tried to lend a hand, Namira stopped her. "No need for you to work. See, this is better." Namira did not want Mery breaking a sweat.

Everyone at Namira's house loved Mery. If she came when they were preparing to have dinner, Samrina insisted she eat with them, even if she had eaten at home. When she did share a meal with the family, Namira's father led grace by saying, "Let us pray according to our respective beliefs." Mery used to chuckle. It reminded her of the closing line at school assemblies on Monday.

Mery liked the tableware at Namira's house. Samrina only brought it out occasionally. The soup tureen had a picture of a snakehead fish and the magenta water pitcher was decorated with a painting of baby shrimps. An old white porcelain plate was used to serve the grilled fish, and they drank from leaf-green glasses with pictures of white reeds. Green plastic bowls filled with water and a wedge of lemon sat ready for washing one's hands.

One item Samrina was most proud of was a flat, white porcelain plate with a black and white picture of an exploding volcano, and the number 1617 on the bottom. It was an antique. Samrina said her grandfather from Banda Eli left it to her. She said it was likely the plate was brought over by his ancestors, who had fled from the Banda Islands to escape the slaughter and slavery in 1621 by Jan Pieterszoon Coen, then governor-general of the Dutch East Indies.

Mery admired more than the tableware. She loved everything about her friend's home: the floors and windows that creaked, the mat made from sago palm fronds, the colorful rolls of cloth in the wooden cupboard, needles stuck in the spools of thread, rags, and strands of thread littering the floorboards.

She knew every inch of Namira's house with its fish baskets, sailing masts, stash of oars, rolled-up sail full of patches, harpoon, net, and cone hat piled in a corner of the kitchen. Floral print curtains hung over the windows, and the yard was planted with lemongrass, a clump of pandan palms and sugarcane, and a noni tree. Their old radio was always tuned to RRI Ternate, playing plaintive Malaysian songs.

The radio was Samrina's every day at ten, when the station played Ebiet G. Ade's songs until noon. The only musician Samrina liked was Ebiet. She liked his poetic lyrics.

Behind the house was a nylon hammock slung between two palm trees, where the girls lolled in the afternoon while listening to the radio, chewing on sugarcane, and enjoying the sea breeze. When the sky turned crimson, Mery helped Namira herd her goat and the ducks into their pens.

Staying over at Namira's house, Mery woke up at the call for the dawn prayer. She waited for Samrina to recite the Qur'an. Mery enjoyed listening to her without knowing why. The Qur'an verses that poured from Samrina mingled with the cold dawn air outside and left her awash in a sense of calm.

Mery would enter the kitchen as soon as Samrina was silent, to find her heating a large pot of water and peeling cassava. Mery enjoyed the sight. It was the same every morning after she had spent the night there. When she tried to help Samrina, Namira took her by the arm to the backyard for counting the dragonflies flitting about the flowers that grew like weeds.

Once, rain and a strong wind from the east bearing down on Elaar caused the entire household to panic. Namira's father shut the windows tight, but they kept opening. Two windows were missing latches. Meanwhile, Samrina cut pieces of cardboard from instant noodle boxes and wedged them between the roof sheaves to block the leaks. She also placed basins through the living room and on the dining table. The sago-leaf roof tended to leak, letting water drip into the house.

Namira did not seem to care. She went to the backyard carrying a lantern, her hair covered with a plastic bag, to check on her goat. She had even given it a name: Famur.

Namira treated the goat like a westerner would a dog. She loved Famur and handfed it banana peels. She spoke to him like Doctor Doolittle to his dog, even though all she received in reply was bleating.

The goat was slaughtered in front of the Al-Hidayah Mosque, a sacrifice for the Eid al-Adha holiday, when Namira was ten years old. Her father had taken the goat early in the morning so she would not see. When she woke up later and went to check on Famur, his pen was empty. She cried and refused to take a bath. She called for Famur on the road, until she found him at the mosque.

Namira wailed and hugged Famur, almost frightening Samrina. The butcher came after the prayer was finished. Namira cried even harder.

Famur was cut into chunks of meat, and Namira refused to speak to anyone. She did not eat and sulked the whole day. She finally stopped moping after Samrina told her the story of Abraham sacrificing his son. But she still asked that Famur be replaced with a sheep. Samrina was annoyed since it was next to impossible to find sheep in Maluku. From that day on, Namira refused to eat goat meat.

Samrina would stop sewing to welcome Mery with open arms every time she came into their house. The soothing smell of shop-fresh textiles and lubricating oil clung to Samrina. She was always oiling her sewing machine so it would hum nicely.

"How are your mother and father?"

"Papa is visiting Letfuar to give tuberculosis treatment counseling." Mery's father, Pieter, was a healthcare worker. He was stocky, with thick sideburns and dark skin, and wore a gold-plated chain as thick as raffia twine. He looked more like a cross between a pimp and a drug dealer than a healthcare worker with a kind heart.

At Mery's house, Namira and her played in the storeroom where Pieter kept his stacks of health brochures and expired family planning packs. He was the only healthcare worker who regularly went to the other islands, and often asked to teach local communities about family planning. Inside the storeroom was a box filled with condoms and intrauterine devices. Namira and Mery took out the condoms and blew them up like balloons or filled them with water.

"And your mother, how is she?" Samrina asked Mery.

"She's busy with her NGO."

As she ladled stew into Mery's bowl, Samrina praised the young girl's mother, Emiliana. "I'm very proud of your mother, Mery. She's a clever woman who is willing to fight for people like us."

For as long as Namira had known her, Emiliana was full of compassion. She worked to improve public education, from developing the skills of the traditional community to taking a stand against the overhunting of sea turtles and sea cucumbers by people outside the Kei islands, which had nearly led to their extinction. Emiliana was constantly immersed in reports and books.

"What would you like for lunch tomorrow? Tube flower stew, melinjo stew, papaya flower stew, or banana blossom stew?" Samrina had asked when the meal was over. "Melinjo stew, Mom." Mery considered Samrina just as much her mother as Emiliana.

If Emiliana were not busy when Namira came to visit, she would watch a movie with the two girls. When *Titanic* was popular and even people in the remotest islands talked about it, Emiliana bought the DVD and watched it with Namira and Mery. When the love scene with Rose and Jack came on, Emiliana grabbed the remote control and fast-forwarded to the next scene.

They also watched *The Old Man and the Sea*, based on the Ernest Hemingway novel. Namira became teary-eyed from the pity she felt for the patient old man who never came home with any fish. Mery had gawked at her friend.

"Watching this movie makes us patient too, as we wait for the old man to finally catch the giant marlin," Namira had said.

Mery was even more perplexed when Namira took her to the Ci Han household goods store to look for a box like the one Manolin used to carry food for the old man. She wanted a box just like Manolin's in the movie.

***

Mery's house was large. In the kitchen, the aluminum sink had a stainless steel faucet. A red sofa with square gray pillows sat in the living room. Several jars filled with candied nutmeg stood on a coffee table covered with a red tablecloth. Pleated curtains covered the windows down to the floor, and an ornamental lamp that looked like a bonfire hung from the ceiling. In another room was a television and bookcase filled with Emiliana and Pieter's books.

At Namira's house, they would sometimes eat from the same plate. Mery was used to eating with utensils at home and had to dig in with her hands. Namira said the food tasted better that way. She said that in Korea people prepared their food without gloves. Touching the food directly with one's hands felt good.

Samrina had said the same thing. The secret to cooking was to touch the spices and the other ingredients.

Mery's mother was rarely in the kitchen. Mery only could turn to Volvot, a rather effeminate man who worked in their house, if there was something special she craved.

When Volvot cooked, he always got angry for no good reason. He would be angry at the faucet for being stuck, or the chicken for spilling coconut oil. Sometimes he cursed a matchstick for going out before he could light the stove.

But none of that bothered Mery because every day Volvot always came up with a different menu.

Volvot came from Depur Island. When Emiliana hosted a small gathering of friends, he made fried fish with sweet soy sauce, or noodle soup with tuna. Mery liked both dishes. She and her mother called him "Miss Volvota," and he liked it. He turned every time he heard the name. Howver, others would call him "Voltage."

Once, Mery was hungry for Samrina's clam soup and asked Volvot to make it. But that was the only dish he never mastered.

Mery often slept alone, her only companion a white stuffed pig with a pink snout. During the long summer school holiday, she would ask her mother to take her to Elaar. She wanted to spend her holidays at Namira's house. If Samrina did not have a lot of sewing, they went to the family's pineapple farm and returned with the fruit to make jam. Samrina would give Mery a jar of pineapple jam when Mery returned to Evu, and sent a jar of jam to Mery's family every Christmas.

When the east wind blew and clamming season began, Namira and Mery went to dig clams. Mery knew Namira's habits. During the full moon, she always had the window in her room opened wide and blew out the oil lamp. Namira and Mery would lie down on the bed to silently look at the moon. Mery sometimes shuddered with the fear someone might jump in the window, but Namira had watched the moon for years. The golden light that arced into the room was always a work of art for her. "It's beautiful," she said and Mery saw the happy expression on her face. Namira certainly was a strange one.

***

Mery flung herself on her bed. Since the conflict started, she had been lonely. Her father was busy with his healthcare work, and her mother visited the refugee camps. Volvot went home at the start of the conflict in Tual. His family came looking for him in Evu. Mery cried and buried her face in her pillow. In her dark room, she thought of Namira's house.

The electricity had gone out a week ago. Nothing came over the radio except the hiss of static. The thought of a mob attacking and killing her while lying in bed suddenly seized her. Mery crawled under her bed. She stayed there until morning.

When she woke up, she found her mother sleeping on the sofa. She must have been very tired. Her father had stayed over at a neighboring island.

Mery went to the kitchen. A bad odor came from the sink. Dirty dishes had piled up over several days. The odor came from rotting vegetables, yams, and fish bones. Mery turned on the faucet. She gathered the food scraps and took them to the bin in the back of the house, and washed the dishes. It was the first time she had done any housework.

Chapter 8

Langgur, May 1999

The wind from the sea was colder than in previous months. Old and young men lined up on the beach. In the distance, a group of three rowboats lit by lanterns snaked their way closer to the shore.

"Everyone get ready." At forty-five, Tinus was the tribal leader's assistant for legal matters. The men held their breath as the rowboats approached. As they drew closer, the sound of the oars churning the water grew clearer. Someone in one of the boats held a lantern aloft and stood up.

"Hey, brothers, we are here," shouted a woman wearing a jilbab.

"Can we come ashore? We have food and clothes for our families taking refuge here," another person in the boat said.

"Yes, my brothers and sisters, you can come ashore," Tinus called out.

Everyone was relieved. They were not attackers or people trying to instigate violence. The latter were out to destabilize Maluku, but on Kei, whether Muslim or Christian, everyone was still a Kei.

The men escorted three of the women from the rowboat to the refugee camp. Once there, they embraced their relatives. "Don't be sad, just calm down. The conflict will end soon and we can be together again. We can't do anything for now, do you understand? This is only temporary." One of the women wiped the tears from her sister's eyes.

The personal ties among the Kei people had always been complex. Many Muslims married Christians, so if a woman was a Muslim, her grandchild could very well be a Christian. A Christian husband could have a Muslim wife, and a Muslim's sibling could be Protestant and their cousin Catholic. That was part of the reason why the Kei were brothers. Their relationships were as complex as the arrangement of the song "Bohemian Rhapsody" by Queen.

In the heart of the Kei lived *snib*—a sacred legacy of the ancestors to always guard, protect, and respect women. Kei men had to protect women everywhere, no matter who they were or what religion they followed. The bringing of food by the women in the rowboats was common in Kei. They knew they would never be hurt.

***

Long before the conflict came to the Kei islands, the people had built churches and mosques together. Catholics, Protestants, and Muslims alike joined in cheerfully. The Kei had a life philosophy: we are all eggs from the same fish and the same bird. Their traditions and tribal laws dated back to historic times, prevailing through the years and superseding all else, including religious doctrine.

When the conflict started in Ambon in January 1999, the Kei stayed calm and refused to take sides. Then on March 31, just before daybreak, violence erupted in Tual. The Kei people learned about it from television and radio reports after the sun had risen high in the sky. Most of them following the developments were convinced the conflict would never leap to the Kei islands. An imam at a mosque said: "The traditional laws of Kei come first. Only after that do people heed the Qur'an or the Bible. The last law we obey is the law of the State of Indonesia."

The conflict was crueler than the angel of death. It spread quickly to the small villages and islands in the area, reaching Elaar and Watraan and other places.

As the conflict escalated, the tribal leaders and settlers—the Buginese, Javanese, Makassarese, Buton, and Chinese—gathered to talk about peace.

***

Namira was trying to calm two young boys at the refugee camp who were arguing and trying to snatch each other's marbles when Sala came along carrying a pair of yellow flip-flops. He knew she had not worn footwear since he first met her, and did not want her stepping on any more glass shards. Since the night at Max's house, Sala's love for Namira had grown by the day. He abandoned his plan of leaving the Kei islands. He wanted the conflict to be over quickly so he could take Namira to Watraan. He wanted to marry her there.

Sala imagined that after a tiring day of forging knives, she would bring him a cup of tea and a plate of fried cassava. His daydreams were filled with the small pleasures of married life. He believed his mother's soul would be at peace if he went back home and revived the metal shop. Namira was all the encouragement he needed.

At lunch at the camp, Namira busied herself preparing Sala's food. It became the talk of everyone working in the kitchen. The volunteers called her and Sala the Romeo and Juliet of Langgur. It annoyed and pleased Namira.

"He's a good man, Ra," said Rohana. She was short and fat, with round cheeks, and always joking and cheerful.

Namira liked Rohana, and so did many of the other refugees. She told funny stories that made the others laugh as though the violence in Kei had never happened.

One day, the volunteers and social workers were upset because the food aid sent by the government had spoiled. The bread was moldy and the instant noodle packets were torn and infested with ants. Seeing the others upset, Rohana started to chatter.

"A young man named Lius went to the same food stall at lunchtime. One day he asked the woman owning the stall, 'Aunty, what stew do you have?'

"The owner said, 'Nail stew, Lius.'

"He ordered the nail stew. The next day he came again at lunchtime. He asked, 'Aunty, what stew do you have?'

"The woman answered, 'Bamboo stew, Lius.'

"Then Lius said, 'Aunty, if this keeps up, tomorrow I'll shit a fence.'"

Another time, when the volunteers were gloomy because of news that the military had entered the conflict in Maluku, Rohana had another funny story to tell. She said that when people complain, things only get worse because the universe repays them with more grief. "So let go and laugh," she said.

The story went like this: A child went home after he was scolded by his teacher at school and told his grandfather. The grandfather became angry and went to the school looking for the teacher. But when he arrived, the teacher had gone home. The grandfather became angrier and went to the teacher's house. He rolled up his sleeves, revealing his tattoos. When he knocked on the teacher's door, a soldier in full uniform answered. The soldier was the teacher's husband. The grandfather suddenly turned coward.

The soldier asked, "Can I help you, pak?"

The grandfather answered, "I wanted to ask the teacher if there was community service at the school today."

Rohana was endearing to Namira, Sala, other volunteers, and the refugees.

***

Sala touched Namira's leg. She woke and rubbed her eyes.

"Sorry." He felt bad waking her up before daybreak.

Namira rose and went to the well. She washed her face and tied her hair back while Sala waited for her. They walked to the ketapang tree and stood so close they formed a single silhouette. Moonlight seeped between the leaves and branches, and fell in a straight line across the ground. Sala pulled Namira into an embrace. He felt uneasy, yet wished he could spend all of his time showing her his love.

A moment later, they headed toward the road and the beach. They walked through patches of beach morning glory and gravel before they reached the white, wet sand. Namira brought a fish basket and Sala carried a set of oars. The village chief's boat was moored on the beach. It was used for fishing so there would be food for the refugees.

"I don't have a good feeling about today. Maybe you should stay on land," Namira said. Besides her premonition, she had a vision of corpses floating on the water and the fish nibbling on them. She shuddered to think people ate the same fish.

Namira looked at Sala, her intuition tied up in knots. She took the fish basket back out of the boat and Sala followed her.

Deep in his heart, he felt the same. Martina had told him that a woman's intuition is stronger than a fortune-teller's prediction.

***

"Not going out to sea today, pela?" a volunteer asked.

"No, Namira won't let me."

When the sun was directly overhead, the sound that had haunted everyone for the past two months returned. It was heard in Elaar, Watraan, and Ngursoin. The refugees scattered. Once again, there was crying and the noise of gunshots. A mob appeared from nowhere and surrounded Langgur, like "rats that suddenly appear from unknown holes, right at the eruption of war."

These unknown rats came with machetes, spears, and arrows. This was the most sorrowful conflict of all—against one's brothers.

A bomb exploded north of Langgur and shook the ground. It felt as though the village would split apart. The refugees ran every direction. Namira could only sit with her wet cheeks and cover her ears. The trauma she experienced in Elaar made her unable to move.

"Those goddamned police and soldiers. Where did these people get their guns if not from them?"

One of the volunteers cursed aloud and added, "This is truly crazy."

Langgur's main street was divided. To the right were the local men and refugees, and to the left the attackers who barricaded the road. The parties threw rocks at each other and the attackers shot arrows that showered the other side like shooting stars.

The road was strewn with rocks. A food kiosk close to Max's house caught fire. Three men lay still on the road. No one helped them. Sala broke through the blockade of men wearing red bandanas. Namira was left behind and hid with another volunteer beside a rusty barrel. A man wearing a red bandana pointed his spear at them.

Namira broke out in a cold sweat.

"Are you Muslim?" he asked.

Namira trembled. The volunteer next to her shut her eyes tight, ready to meet her barbaric end with dignity.

"Hey, pela, don't you hurt those girls or you'll get hurt yourself." A voice like a tiger's roar pierced Namira's ears. Sala stood in front of the man with the red bandana. "I won't fight you, pela. I don't want to give those seeking bloodshed any reasons to cheer."

Namira looked intently at Sala.

The volunteer babbled, "Oh, Allah, Jesus, Elohim, Hallelujah, Dalai Lama, gods of the sky, bring peace to Kei."

Sala stepped up to the man with the spear.

"I'm the same as you, I have the same religion. But if we join in the slaughter, we'll only satisfy those who want to see chaos in Maluku," Sala said.

It was like a miracle. The man with the red bandana was quiet. He had only been paid to do something that he was reluctant to do. Sala pulled Namira by the arm. She collapsed in his embrace, sobbing. "Please find Esme," she said between tears.

***

Black smoke blanketed Langgur and the other villages, resembling a flock of crows passing overhead. The stench of death was like the scent of frangipani at night. The refugees who were still alive fled in boats along with the women and children of the village. This time they headed to Evu.

Sala asked Namira to go there too. He had to remain in Langgur with the other men and protect the village. They planned to secure the public facilities so the village did not have the same fate as the one on the other island—it was best not to mention the name out of decency and horror. The well in that village, the people's only source of fresh water, was filled with severed body parts. The stench was overwhelming.

The unrest had caused many horrors, stories of corpses without arms or legs, or heads or shoulders or chests. One report from an island to the south reached Langgur, about a gunnysack being found behind the mosque filled with the body of a man and swarming with fat maggots.

***

Namira gazed at Sala with tears in her eyes. She jumped out of the boat and hugged him, crying. Sala held her tight and stroked her hair. He shed a teardrop. It held sadness more profound than the most hysterical crying.

"Go, wait in Evu. Don't worry. I'll find you. The conflict will soon wear itself out. I love you."

Sala peeled Namira's arms from his waist and took her to the boat. Once on the water, sea foam lapped at its hull. A sea eagle soared in the sky above Langgur, returning to its nest. Below the bird were people without hope of being reunited with their families.

Namira stared at the yellow flip-flops on her feet. They looked like the sign of a long journey ahead of her.

Far away, Sala stood on the beach.

Chapter 9

Evu, May 1999

Mery hugged Namira and kept saying, "Sorry." The two frightened girls sobbed together.

When Emiliana heard on the radio that fighting had broken out in Langgur, she asked Mery and Orlando, her younger brother, to quickly go and get Namira. Their boats crossed in the middle of the sea.

Mery felt bad that she had been late in picking up her friend. Namira and four other women and their children moved to Orlando's boat. They were all silent and grieving. One of the women threw up. Namira sat downwind and was almost hit in the face by it.

They passed another boat, carrying humanitarian volunteers to Langgur. They were going to defuse the tension, and prevent the conflict from spreading like a cholera epidemic.

"I heard the volunteers and tribal elders are going to stop the conflict through the power of *ken sa faak*," Mery said, breaking the silence and the tension.

"We must pray it works," Orlando said. Namira and the others nodded in unison.

"Where are you from?" a woman asked Namira.

"From Elaar, ibu."

"I know an Uncle Hasan there. I wonder how he is." she said, quietly.

"I do not know, ibu."

"This trouble has caused us to lose touch with those we love. It's hard to find out what has happened to them," another woman said.

A third woman joined the conversation. She spoke of a young boy named Ali in the village of Faan. On the night the attackers struck the village, he was at a friend's house watching television. His uncle rushed to look for him and found the house had been razed in a fire. "His mother and a younger sibling died in the flames," the woman said.

Four years earlier, fighting had broken out between the people of the Upper Hollat and Lower Hollat at the foot of a mountain on Kei Besar. For months, the two villages just a few hundred yards apart attacked one another. The battle stemmed from a dispute over their borders at sea. Fighting between two villages was always a very sensitive issue because under Kei law, fighting to defend one's territory was acceptable.

Peace was achieved only through ken sa faak. It started with *fnevh nuh*, a ritual to cleanse each village of the violations committed there. After the ritual, an oath of peace was sworn.

***

"How is Aunt Emili?" Namira asked.

"She can't sleep and works even harder. I feel sorry for her. Yesterday she took medical aid to Toyando Island."

"And Uncle Pieter?"

"Father and the other volunteers built a medical post at the village of Dian."

"May God repay their goodness," Namira exhaled slowly, thinking about Sala.

***

It was close to midnight when the boat reached the shore near Evu. A team of volunteers waited to take the refugees straight to a shelter. Evu's main street was lined with different kinds of posts: a volunteer post, an indigenous peoples post, and those set up by foreign organizations.

The wounded poured into Evu. A man on a stretcher screamed from the gashes in his thigh and shoulder. Volunteers carried him into a medical tent, where they bandaged his wounds. The smell of boric acid wafted from the open tent.

***

Mery's house was quiet as usual. Namira immediately lay down on the sofa.

"I'm really sorry Mama and Papa have not found out anything more about your mother," Mery said.

"You've tried more than anyone else."

"Stay with me for now. We have to be careful because there has been talk the attackers are threatening any Catholic who is hiding a Muslim." Mery walked to the kitchen and went on, "I don't know when the conflict started including the Kei people. It has divided and pitted us against each other."

She returned to the living room with a bowl of bean porridge for Namira. Since the conflict had swept across Kei, Mery had rarely seen Namira's usual cheerful expression. She understood that Namira's soul was torn. Part of her wanted to look for her mother, while another part stayed in Langgur with the wavy-haired young man.

Namira brought a spoonful of the steaming porridge to her lips. Her eyes met the painting hanging in front of her, "The Last Supper." The bearded men in the painting appeared to be enjoying their meal in peace at that long table. It was a stark contrast to her situation.

"Don't dwell too much on your mother, Ra. We should pray and keep praying."

Namira nodded in agreement.

"Rest a while. I'm going to the volunteer post and help with registering the refugees. When you feel better, you can join me. But for now just lie down."

The house felt empty once Mery was gone. Namira looked around her friend's room. It was the same as when she came over during the school holidays.

She looked at the wooden shelf that held a stuffed pig, dog, and panda. A plastic Hello Kitty frame held a photograph of the two girls taken after scout practice. Emiliana had made them stand in front of the fence and strike a pose embracing each other. Namira and Mery looked like clowns, their faces smeared with lipstick and blush. Namira smiled.

Her gaze traveled to a card taped on the wall. Namira recognized the cursive writing on the card. It was Mery's handwriting. She read:

"Love is patient, love is kind. It does not envy, it does not boast, it is not proud. It is not rude, it is not self-seeking, it is not easily angered, it keeps no record of wrongs. Love does not delight in evil but rejoices with the truth. It always protects, always trusts, always hopes, always perseveres. Love never fails."

Namira loved Mery. They were like sisters. Both were an only child and had bound themselves to each other with the ties of sisterhood since grade school. Mery's father used to work in Elaar. The two families were next-door neighbors. Since they were little, the girls had never fought.

She was deeply saddened when Mery's father took a job in Evu and the family had to move. Namira cried louder as a boat carried away the family's furniture.

***

Emiliana returned home early. She immediately hugged Namira, who let her body sink into the embrace. The great thing about a fat woman was that her hugs were always warm and motherly. Emiliana and Namira wept.

"I'm so sorry, child. I still haven't found out about your mother." Namira had heard the same words from Mery, and now she heard them from Emiliana. They were still talking when Mery came home with a look of exasperation. She gulped a glass of water and put a hand on her hip.

"Many of the refugees are sick and we don't have nearly enough medicine. We're out of diarrhea medicine, aspirin, slings, and bandages. Many of the wounded refugees complain that the medications do nothing to stop their pain," Mery said.

"There was a woman trying to give birth in tent number two. The baby would not come out. Everyone was worried, but what made me upset was how the midwife acted. She was like a director angry with her underlings. If we had four midwives on this island I would have poisoned this one by now." Mery wrung her hands as she spoke.

"It is too bad Father is not back yet from Dian," she added.

"What did the midwife do?" asked Namira.

"She kept swearing the whole time she was giving instructions to the woman. Incredibly stupid," Mery spat out.

The story reminded Namira of her mother. Each time they went into the forest, her mother would point out various plants and their medicinal properties.

"Look, Namira, that is *dailokoh*. The leaves can cure boils. Look closely at the shape of the leaves, child." It pleased Samrina to see Namira holding and studying the plant. A few yards further on, Samrina said, "Now this one, child, is *ladeh*. Our ancestors used to use this to treat internal injuries." Pointing at a tree a few hundred meters away, she said, "This one is important for you, because when you are pregnant and about to give birth, boil the young leaves of the *galatoda* tree and drink the water. It will make the delivery easier."

When the memory of the galatoda tree came back to Namira, she grabbed Mery by the hand and they went into the woods of Evu. The heat of the day dissipated beneath the cover of the trees. The girls searched for the plants they needed to ease the woman's labor.

They peeled bark from the *gwaya* and *posi-posi* trees, and picked leaves from the *gumrucai* and *balacai*, everything a pregnant woman needed. Namira boiled the galatoda leaves at Mery's house, and the two friends returned to the camp. The midwife's rude exhortations could be heard outside the tent.

"Come on, take a breath and push. Come on. Push harder. You were quiet when making the baby, why cry to get it out? Come on, push. Quit being a crybaby."

The pregnant woman was upset. The midwife did not understand how difficult it was for a woman to give birth in a refugee camp, especially with her spread legs in clear view of people walking by.

"Push. Don't cry." The more the midwife encouraged the woman, the more upset she became.

Namira was incensed as she stood behind the midwife. She had likely bribed her way into school and fooled around when she should have been studying. Namira supposed the midwife must have gone to one of those unaccredited academies. She suspected she only wanted to be a midwife so people would call her a healthcare worker.

The midwife grew weary and turned away to prepare an injection to induce labor.

Namira went to the pregnant woman bathed in sweat and whispered, "I brought you a glass of boiled galatoda water. Just drink this. My mother said this eases the pain of childbirth."

The midwife stared in disbelief as the skinny girl, who did not look like she had any midwife training, brought a glass to the woman's lips.

Early the next morning Mery flung herself on the bed beside Namira and hugged her. "Praise be to God, she has given birth," she said.

Namira was elated. Her thoughts flew back to her mother. Samrina had always relied on the leaves from the forest whenever anyone in the family fell sick. Long before the leaves of the *binahong* plant became popular for treating burns, acne, bloating, and impotence, Samrina knew about its many benefits.

Samrina had passed down her knowledge of herbs to Namira.

***

In life, there are things one cannot control: floods, tsunamis, and drought are among them. But the Kei elders and volunteers knew they could control the conflict through the wisdom of ken sa faak, which in the Kei language meant, "We are all at fault."

Namira sat on a palm-frond mat outside a tent and was telling the children the Kei folk tale, "Lateo and the Dolphins" when Rohana arrived.

It moved her to see the young girl take on the children's sadness. She let Namira finish the story before she joined her. Namira put her arms around Rohana. She always managed to spark hope in Namira because of their time together in Langgur.

She wanted to know about Sala right away. "Is he alright?" Namira whispered as she hugged Rohana.

"Romeo of Langgur is just fine. He said to give this to you," she said, blowing Namira a kiss.

"I mean, he's not hurt, right?"

"No, don't worry, Namira. He's fine. He and the young men of Langgur are taking part in the peace efforts."

Namira heaved a sigh of relief.

"He sent a letter for you. I'm going to my tent." Rohana handed her a white envelope.

Namira's hands shook as she unfolded the letter.

> *For Namira in Evu,*
> *I have missed you since the moment you stepped*
> *into the boat that took you to Evu. Max says*
> *I have been like someone with hepatitis since*
> *you left. I am listless, he says.*
>
> *Last night we all sat down together, the*
> *young men, tribal elders, and activists, and*

talked about bringing peace to this mess. You have no idea how hard that is. The problem is that the source of the conflict is not something we are familiar with. It is not about defending a woman's honor or defending one's territory. At the meeting yesterday, Menkem Esomar, a humanitarian activist, said that the conflict was not started by the Kei people, but instigated by an outside influence and the violence in Kei is just a consequence.

Ah, Namira, what mad times we live in. The officials are busy robbing and partying, while the people in the regions suffer and are killed. The forests are raped by fire, babies are hit by taxes before they are born, and religious people act like Pharisees. But what is most important is that you are safe over there.

I'm okay right now. Every day I pray that you are always healthy too. We must get married as soon as this unrest ends. I can't stand being apart for much longer.

I have some happy news. Esme, the woman you came with to Langgur, has evacuated to Dian. She is safe and her child is healthy.

Sala

P.S. I miss you. I miss you. I miss you. I miss you. I miss you. I miss you one hundred times.

The words blurred as Namira read each "I miss you." She folded the letter and put it in the pocket of her skirt. A little girl with her hair in a ponytail came up to her and hugged her from behind.

"Was that letter from your boyfriend?" she asked.

"Ahhh," Namira drew a long breath, her cheeks flushed.

"Where's your boyfriend from?"

"He's from Watraan, my dear."

"What religion are you?"

"I'm Muslim, my dear."

"And your boyfriend?"

"He's Protestant, my dear."

"Are you allowed to date when you have different religions?"

The question left Namira speechless; she did not know how to answer.

"Why do you stay quiet? Are you allowed to or not?" the girl asked again.

Namira knelt down and placed her hands on the girl's shoulders. "God is the one who decides in matters of love. We can't choose where to place our heart. The heart makes its own choice. Do you understand, my dear?" The girl shook her head.

"You will when you are older. Now, get ready to take a bath. We are going to play *sife siflyoi* very soon."

The girl ran into the tent and came out carrying a small towel and a water dipper with her toiletries inside.

Namira gathered the girls of the refugee camp. Sife siflyoi was meant to teach them about togetherness, sharing, responsibility, hard work, and friendship.

The children were soon busy picking the teams. The game had two teams: the eagle team went after the chicken team, which had to protect itself and its chicks. Each team had the same number of players.

"Diana, do you want to be in the eagle team or the chicken team?"

"The eagle team," said Diana, a tall, thin girl. Her hair was burnt red by the sun. She rarely smiled and sometimes cried at seeing a sharp object. Her father was beheaded before her eyes. Her mother, who was cooking in the kitchen at the time, jumped up and tried to shield her. Mother and child fled through the window. They were refugees from Letfuar, a village north of Evu.

"Saida, what team do you want to be in?"

"Eagle."

"You're too fat for the eagle team. If you run into us, we'll pass out," the other girls protested.

"Hush. Don't act like that to your friend. Saida, would you like to be a mother hen? Protecting your friends is a noble job."

Saida nodded and Namira patted her head. The girl came from the village of Larat, and the village was truly miserable after the violence had swept through. She was ten but big for her age. She scratched her head every few seconds. A bad case of lice had left her scalp dotted with festering sores that gave off a bad odor.

The previous week one of the girls, Yeti, saw Saida suffer from her itchy scalp, and had the others rub insecticide chalk over Saida's head. "That way the lice get intoxicated," Yeti told Namira.

Once the girls were assigned to a team, they sang to mark the start of the game:

> *Tuk tuk tuk nurlolofu keta kune.*
> Hey little chicks, hide under your
>   mother's wings.
> *Oka siflyoi uma nbotin nuse tubun*
> If you do not
> *Ino we metriat.*
> The eagle will catch you.

Namira laughed as she watched the eagles take on the hens until Mery arrived out of breath.

"Ra, six motorboats full of refugees are on the beach and every tent is occupied. You have to help me, Ra. We have to get them to a shelter, especially the children."

They raided Emiliana's cupboards for every blanket they could find, and handed them out. The newly arrived refugees soon crowded into Mery's living room, where they slept packed together. In Mery's room, the children jostled for space on the bed.

After the refugees had fallen asleep, Namira and Mery looked at each other. The sight of the fifty-odd people crammed into the living room had them worried.

***

In the middle of the night, Pieter knocked loudly on the door, calling for Emiliana and Mery.

"Quickly pack everything you need. We're leaving right now," he said as soon as Emiliana opened the door. He stopped when he saw the refugees in his living room, squeezed together like sardines in a can.

Pieter carefully stepped over the bodies to fetch a large bag from the cupboard, and filled it with important documents. Emiliana joined him under the dim light of the oil lamp. Nearly five minutes passed before Pieter spoke.

"What are these people doing here?" he whispered.

"The camp is full. The refugees have been pouring in since Langgur fell to the violence. Mery brought them here."

"We have to get out this very night."

"Why the rush?"

"We don't have much time. A friend of mine offered us passage on his freight ship to Makassar."

Emiliana was insistent about staying. "We aren't leaving Evu, Pieter. Kei is our land. We can't leave when things are this bloody."

"I don't want my family to be slaughtered, Emili. I'm tired of seeing all the dead." He sat down and ran his hands through his hair.

Emiliana knew she should be angry with him for his sudden decision, but a voice inside told her it was better to act wisely and gently.

In the dark, surrounded by the sleeping refugees, she took her husband's hand and held it tight. She leaned her head on his shoulder.

Pieter told her about the rotting organs he had seen, the broken limbs and chopped fingers. He told her about the slashed throats, stab wounds, cracked skulls, and faces seared by fire. Pieter wept as he spoke.

"You know what the Kei women have always been like. We have a role to play in ending the war," Emiliana said. "Do you see these people in our house? They need us. The conflict has made us hate one another, and lose our trust and become saddened. The one thing we must maintain is our conscience, our sense of compassion. Don't ever let this war take away your compassion."

Emiliana kept talking to her husband, with her voice as low as possible.

Pieter hugged her. As a father and husband, his instinct was to keep his family out of harm's way. But his wife had always been a fighter, and was a humanitarian activist long before Pieter decided to propose marriage. He had known what it would be like to marry a woman like Emiliana.

"The last news I heard was that the people of Warwut have plans to attack Evu. I hope this only a rumor. But if it happens, I have prepared everything. I need your support. I need you by my side," Emiliana said, trying to convince her husband.

When she heard of the impending assault, Emiliana's instinct as an activist was to prevent it. She called the wife of the village chief. If the attackers came to Evu, the women would meet them carrying betel leaves and areca nuts. For years, the leaves and nuts had been potent symbols for seeking peace in Kei.

***

Three days later, the rumor proved true. The attackers overwhelmed the small group of Evu youths guarding the border of the village. Unrest in Maluku sent ripples of violence through the small islands. The attackers shouted and waved their machetes and bamboo spears. They struck with brutality. The same fate that had befallen Langgur, Elaar, and Watraan had spread to Evu.

Pieter stood in the street shouting for Emiliana, Mery, and Namira. An ethnic Chinese businessman from Ambon, the owner of the freighter *Cinta Semusim* that often visited Makassar to pick up textiles and food, offered passage for anyone who could make it down to the beach.

Namira was cleaning fish nearby when she heard a scream that froze her legs. Every time Namira had been too petrified to move, God had always sent someone good to her. This time it was an old woman wearing a jilbab. She took Namira by the arm and pulled her on board the ship.

A cloud of black smoke rose from the other end of the village, and the freighter left Evu. Namira was headed to Makassar along with hundreds of ethnic Buginese and Buton traders. They had lost all hope. Their shops and stores in Tual had been reduced to rubble. Now they returned to the land of their birth.

The old woman who had guided Namira to the ship had mistaken her for the daughter of a friend, a rice vendor.

***

In Evu, the attackers seized control of one quarter of the village. Their blood boiled with rage as Emiliana and other women marched into the center of the mob with offerings of betel leaves and areca nuts. The attackers were stunned and dropped their weapons in a single movement. They knew the laws of Kei: accept the leaves and nuts and eat them as a sign of peace.

Their steps no longer as sure, the attackers turned back. The Kei tradition buried in their hearts was stronger than anything else. Even in the heat of a fight, they had to stop when a woman intervened. Women were a symbol of the tradition, and the men a symbol of the ancestors. They should never cause a woman to shed a tear because her tears were gold. When the men had calmed down and the fire in their eyes extinguished, Mery and Pieter went to Emiliana and hugged her.

Emiliana looked around. "Where is Namira?" The relief on their faces vanished.

Mery plunged into the crowd looking for Namira and could not find her.

Emiliana searched in the tents of the refugee camp, but there was no trace of the girl.

***

Out in the middle of the sea, Namira sat on the deck of the ship and leaned against a wall. Her bones felt as if they had detached from her joints. She cursed her legs for never being able to move when she was scared. Images flashed before her eyes: Emiliana's warm embrace, the ever-attentive Mery.

Namira sobbed. She imagined being held by a young man. She imagined Sala searching the streets of Evu, asking people where she was and not being able to find her.

She looked at the yellow flip-flops on her feet. She picked them up and pressed them to her chest.

Chapter 10

Langgur, June 1999

News of the fighting in Evu reached Sala. He ran to the health clinic in Langgur, hoping to get on the radio to Evu. But the radio was not working.

Max tried to quiet his friend's anxiety. "Just calm down. Tomorrow when my father gets back from Dian we'll go to Evu by speedboat. Try not to think too much. Namira is bound to be alright."

"I'm worried about her," Sala said.

Max patted Sala on the back. "I know."

Sala was unable to close his eyes that night. His mind was focused on Namira, trapped in Evu. He got up, smoked, strummed his guitar, lay down, smoked again, and lay down again. His eyes refused to stay shut. He finished a pack of cigarettes.

Max shook his head. "You are really in love with that Muslim girl."

"It's not a matter of her being Muslim, Hindu, Buddhist, or Christian. This is about her life." Sala shocked Max with his irate reaction.

"Relax, pela. I wasn't mocking Namira for being Muslim, honestly. I'm sorry, I just misspoke."

Sala was silenced by his sadness.

***

The cold of the previous night clung to the gray morning as the speedboat cut through the water, leaving a foamy wake. On either side, wind rattled the palm tree leaves in the island groves. The two young men remained silent. The boat beached near Evu around noon. Sala jumped into the shallows and ran to the shore before Max had turned off the engine.

"Who are you?" asked a man on the beach.

"We're from Langgur, pak. I'm Max and this is my friend, Sala. We're looking for a friend of ours."

Sala ran to the refugee camp and checked every tent for the face he missed so much. Namira was not there, only the grieving who stared back at him in a daze.

"Do you know a woman called Namira?" Sala checked with each of the refugees. They all shook their heads.

Meanwhile Max tried to stay calm and talked to the man on the beach. He held out his hand and apologized.

Sala came back to him looking distraught. "She's not here."

"I thought you said Namira had a friend in Evu."

"Yes, Mery."

Max and Sala asked people for Mery's address. When they knocked on the teak door of the large brick house, Mery opened the door, warily.

"I know you. Is Namira here?" Sala asked.

"We lost her. When the riot broke out here, she was at the beach. I think she boarded the freighter with other refugees," Mery said in a low voice. "Maybe she didn't want to be a burden to us."

Sala felt weak. He and Max left Mery's house.

Sala stopped people they passed on the road. "Do you know Namira Evav?"

Some shook their heads. Others did not answer. Some nodded. A few people recognized her name. "Oh sure, I know her. The sweet girl who is a storyteller, right? She tells folk tales to the refugee children."

***

Back on the beach, Sala sat down. His chest ached.

Max was silent. His friend was truly miserable. "Love always finds its own way, pela," he said.

Chapter 11

Makassar, January 2001

Namira moved her gaze from the jewelry store across the street to the chicken noodle diner packed with people, and back again. In her hand, she clutched the gold chain from Esme.

Her lips were dry and her head ached from not having eaten all day. She had worked as a waitress in a grilled fish restaurant until the owner pinched her cheek when they were alone in the kitchen. She quit.

Namira stepped into the jewelry store. The man behind the counter looked at her with suspicion.

"I want to sell my chain," Namira said.

The storeowner signaled the man behind the counter.

He took the chain and weighed it. "The chain is one and a half grams. The pendant is one gram. Two and a half grams in all."

"How much is a gram of gold worth?" Namira asked.

"Eighty thousand. But for a used item like this we can only pay fifty thousand," the storeowner said.

"So, one hundred and twenty-five thousand?"

"Yes," the storeowner said.

Namira handed over the chain. As she left the store, she silently asked God to bless Esme for her generosity. She entered the diner she had watched all day and ordered a bowl of chicken noodles.

At the end of the long bench where Namira waited, a girl was drawing. She occasionally glanced at a woman with straight hair, almond eyes, and fair skin. When the girl finished the drawing, Namira called out to her. "Order something and I'll pay."

"I'm not hungry, thank you, but you go ahead."

"Come on, eat with me. Never turn down a free meal," Namira said. She had recognized the girl as one of the street artists who often sat outside the grilled fish restaurant where she had worked.

Namira kept insisting. Finally, she asked for an avocado smoothie.

"What's your name?" the girl asked Namira.

"Namira, and you?"

"Kumala," she said, sipping her smoothie.

"Where do you live?"

"In a boarding house near the muddy canal," Namira grimaced.

"Where are your parents?"

"They died in the conflict." Namira's eyes filled with tears. "I mean, my father died. I don't know what happened to my mother."

"You have a gray aura about your face from holding too much sadness," Kumala said.

"Really? Can you read people's auras?" Namira was curious. Kumala seemed to have her own quirks.

Kumala did not answer. Instead, she asked more questions.

"So, do you work here?"

"It's funny, you're like a reporter," Namira laughed and Kumala joined her.

"I used to work at the grilled fish restaurant, but I quit. The owner was a jerk."

"Do you want to stay with me?" Kumala's question caused Namira to choke on her food. Kumala pushed a glass of water toward her. They barely knew each other and already she was offering her a place to stay. She was too good. "Kindness is everywhere for the kind-hearted," Samrina had once told her.

"Who do you live with?"

"I live with my mother. It's just the two of us."

Namira searched for truth in Kumala's eyes. The clear lakes only reflected kindness and sincerity.

***

Namira was startled when they arrived at the gate of Kumala's house. This girl who went from diner to diner drawing pictures did not come from a struggling family. She lived in a 1950s-style house surrounded by a tall fence.

Nana, Kumala's mother, owned the Keumala Store. She sold old knickknacks, from porcelain dice to teak doors with carved dragons and *hong* birds.

"Come in," Kumala said cheerfully. "My mother is at the store. We'll go and see her."

Kumala's mother dressed like a gypsy in her long, lace-fringed skirt. She wore her jilbab so it showed off her dangling earrings. When she held out her hand, bracelets clattered on her wrist. "Nana," said the beautiful woman.

Namira guessed she was in her forties.

"My mother opened her store because she says the older these things get, the more valuable they become. Even though she doesn't sell as much as other stores, there are always people who miss the past, and they look for old things.

"Besides, fashion and taste always circle back to the past," Kumala added, as though she could tell what Namira was thinking.

Namira looked around her admiringly. On a table sat a copper-toned gramophone with a hand crank. Nearby stood a stack of records and Osaka jars. On the wall was a glass-fronted painting of the *wayang* characters—Semar, Petruk, Gareng, and Bagong—wittily rendered flying in a *kamikaze* plane. Close by the painting hung four maps of Indonesia, also in glass frames, from 1927.

"That map is originally from the book, *Kleine Schoolatlas Van Nederlandsch Oost Indie, Denhaag Weltevreden*," Kumala said as she saw Namira look at the maps.

"What? *Klin skolas van nederlan os indi,*" Namira stammered, trying to repeat what Kumala said.

"Oh, never mind. You'll get your tongue tied up in knots if you try to pronounce it properly."

Namira turned to the wooden shelf at the left side of the store, where two Siegfried Gross tube radios were displayed. She stroked the wood cases of the old radios and thought of her creaky house and their National radio. She and Mery often fought over which station to listen to, and laughed at the presenters with their strange, stilted names: Putri Bunga Bakung (Lily Princess), Pangeran Merana (Pining Prince), Putra Kelelawar (Bat Prince), Putri Halilintar (Lightning Princess), Putri Cerewet (Nagging Princess), Putri Manis Manja (Sweet Spoiled Princess), and Putra Petir (Lightning Prince).

"The wood and tubes are still in prime condition," Nana said.

Namira was dazzled. Walking into Nana's store was like stepping into a museum. Old-fashioned rooster lamps hung from the ceiling. Pushed against the wall on the right were four Kohler sewing machines, straight from the factory in Altenburg.

"These sewing machines use a crank, not a pedal like the machines these days," Kumala explained as she turned the handle on the right side of one of the machines. Two antique sideboards and an old piano stood next to the sewing machines.

"The piano was made at the M. Schulz factory in Chicago. Do you know when the factory was built?"

Kumala asked, as though she was posing a question on a TV quiz show.

Namira shook her head.

"In 1869," Kumala said proudly. "The piano isn't for sale. It's only here for show. It was a birthday present from my late father," she explained, like she was talking to a buyer.

Next to the cashier's desk, a glass china cabinet displayed a jade pebble, a Buginese dagger, a Rolex from the 1970s, a miniature Qur'an, and a Bible in ancient Javanese script. Everything in the store reminded Namira of her mother's old porcelain plates.

Over the following days, Namira helped at the store. Most of the people who came in just looked around. Namira enjoyed her new role as storekeeper.

For Kumala, an only child, there was the pleasure of a friend at home other than her mother.

Namira loved Kumala the way she loved Mery. It amazed her how she managed to strike up friendships with only children. Mery was an only child, and so was Sala. Children without siblings have so much love to give and don't know who to share it with, she thought.

Kumala shared with Namira her taste in music, clothes, and books. When she played Namira a song by the Beatles or Chrisye, Namira immediately liked it.

***

On Friday, January 19, Namira went with Kumala to a mall. As she passed by a television display, she stopped. The news anchor talked about the situation in Ambon.

"An exchange of gunfire occurred between the military and police in the early hours at Batu Merah. In the incident, a joint battalion of the Marines, Army Special Forces, and Air Force Special Forces shot dead a police officer and fifteen Muslim residents seeking refuge in a shop-house in Batu Merah, Sirimau, Ambon. Meanwhile, the Pattimura XVI military commander, I Made Suhasta, said he had not ordered the firing. That's the breaking news for now. Stay tuned."

The conflict in Maluku dragged on. The government, it seemed, was powerless to stop the violence. The deaths in Maluku were just statistics.

Namira gasped. She ran down the escalator for the toilet and threw up.

Chapter *12*

Banda Sea, August 2001

Under the wan starlight, the Banda Sea appeared like a giant bowl. Five thousand meters under the surface was a tangle of trenches, connecting deep troughs to shallower ones. Part of the Banda Sea lay against the Pacific Ocean. The ship, *Bukit Siguntang,* held over a thousand refugees, and cut through the choppy water past imposing coral reefs. In the distance, the hills on land were only silhouettes.

Sala sat on the deck of the ship lost in his sadness. He tried to bury his disappointment at not having found Namira in Evu by going to Jakarta. His friend Edo had promised him a job. Even so, his feelings remained unsettled. Nothing was certain anymore. His dream of returning to Watraan and reviving the metal workshop his grandfather had built dissolved in the froth of the waves, scattering into nothingness. Sala felt like driftwood floating in no certain direction.

He had imagined living with Namira, their wedding, and their baby. Those hopes were crushed in Evu. Skyscrapers, movie theaters, and glass-walled stores might salve his bitterness. He had no idea what Jakarta was like.

He wondered if the vastness of Jakarta was like the dangers of the ocean to the newly hatched turtle—full of sharks, giant groupers, and killer whales. Jakarta, the sparkling city of countless dreams, also had the power to bring anyone down.

Sala plucked his guitar and sang sad songs. Everything about Namira appeared before him like a series of pictures: sitting with her under the ketapang tree, her telling all sorts of stories, giving her the pair of flip-flops; standing with her as they washed dishes at the spring outside the church; pulling the sliver of glass from her foot; and the moment they became one.

"Daydreaming again?" Edo appeared with a bottle of Coca-Cola and a pack of cigarettes. "I'm hungry. We should go to the pantry."

"I'm not hungry."

"You'll get seasick if you don't eat. Come with me."

Sala ignored Edo. He refused the drink and cigarettes Edo held out to him.

"There are more women, Sala. Just wait until we get to Jakarta. Beautiful women are everywhere: cleaners, trash pickers, ticket vendors, they are all beautiful."

Sala had lost his appetite since leaving Evu. Love hurt far more than he had imagined. Namira was the first girl he had given his heart to, and in turn she had bared her thoughts to him.

Sala and Edo were at sea for five days and nights. When the ship docked at Tanjung Priok Port, they were picked up by a bespectacled man with skin as dark as asphalt and curly hair. His name was Markus.

***

Everyone in Jakarta knew Yohanes, the man from Southeast Maluku who had a hand in the violence in the capital. Markus introduced Sala to Yohanes. His underlings called him Boss Yo. He knew Jakarta like every line and curve of the tattoos that covered his arms and legs. Although he lived in Jakarta, his name was known in the most far-flung islands of Southeast Maluku. Yohanes headed an organization of youths from Tual, called the Nyong Muda Kei Organization, or ONMI, which was formed after the conflict reached Southeast Maluku.

Sala was recruited as a member. At first he thought he would be put to work as a security guard at a hotel or bank, because at ONMI he was trained in self-defense using a gun, a bow and arrow, and a machete. He wondered what kind of job would require him to master these various weapons. Would he be assigned as a security guard at a housing estate or an office building? For months, it remained a mystery.

One night he finally decided to ask Edo.

"What are we actually hired for? Why are we taught to use those weapons? I'm sure you would never get me in trouble."

Edo looked at him and was silent for a moment. He said, "What kind of work did you expect to do in Jakarta? All we have are high school diplomas. Jakarta is overflowing with people who have master's degrees and doctorates from overseas. There are not enough jobs for them in the government or private offices. Last night we saw those women at the traffic light, selling their bodies. You've never seen anything like that in Kei, have you?"

Sala let his mind wander. He was certain there were jobs out there that did not require the skills of using deadly weapons.

***

Sala was trained to be a debt collector and a menace for the more belligerent debtors. Boss Yo would gather his men when there was a request to guard a plot of land under dispute, or a bar or pub or nightclub required ONMI's services. At a minimum cost of one hundred million rupiah, the services did not come cheap. In addition to debt collection, Boss Yo also provided contract killing. The debt collection racket had been around for a while. Before Boss Yo, Johnny Sembiring controlled it. He was killed at the Matraman intersection in 1966, and the business fell to Hercules. In 1990, Boss Yo muscled into the game, competing directly with Hercules.

Boss Yo sat in a leopard-print chair in a cheap club. He always chose that kind of club for security, since his rivals and reporters rarely frequented them. Only stupid or poor policemen showed up.

He had his back turned to Sala and Edo. Markus put a clove cigarette to Boss Yo's lips. He flicked a lighter, his body hunched over, as Sala looked on amused.

"Sala," Boss Yo called out. Many of his men broke into a cold sweat in his presence.

Sala stepped closer.

"Kill this man. His name is Abraham." Boss Yo showed him a photograph.

Sala shivered at the words from Boss Yo. The order to kill someone seemed so casual, as though all he had asked Sala to do was fetch him a beer. Sala looked at Edo.

His friend looked down. Edo could not bear to look into Sala's wounded eyes.

"The Kei ancestors taught us never to take a life. You know that amounts to *Nevnev*," Sala said anxiously. "We follow the seven articles of Nevnev, the Law of Transgression."

Boss Yo calmly looked at him. "Nevnev? Cut the crap," he said, his expression impossible to read.

Sala cited the sayings of the ancestors, talking like he was possessed. He had seen too much death during the conflict in Kei and did not want to see more.

"Don't lecture me about the ancestors' sayings. In Jakarta they have no meaning."

"If the teachings are violated, the ancestors and God will never forgive us. Misfortune will follow on land, sea, and air. I won't kill anyone. Ever." Sala's face turned red.

Boss Yo shouted for Markus, his voice flat. "Take Sala back to the base. He is not ready to be an ONMI member." He referred to the large house where his men lived and trained as "the base." Senior members made enough to rent or buy their own homes. As Sala was bustled out of the club, Boss Yo told Markus to watch him.

Sala felt the barrel of a gun against his back. "Keep walking and don't try anything funny," Markus said.

***

Sala was caged like a prisoner in a stuffy room lit by a twenty-watt bulb. Deep disappointment ate at his chest. He had trusted Edo as a comrade in the shared struggle away from home, and Edo turned out to be a hammerhead shark—one that ate its own kind in the depths of the ocean. Edo had preyed on his own brother from the same people and land.

As a child, Sala had dreamed of going to Jakarta when he was older. The people from his village who went to Jakarta always returned with the most wonderful stories. They spoke of the malls with stairs powered by machines, towering buildings, playgrounds, celebrities they passed in the malls, and many other stories. He listened to everything, wondering when he would get a chance to go.

The Jakarta of his childhood was a dream, a land in the middle of nowhere, and he only saw its wonders on his neighbor's black-and-white television. Now that he was finally here, the dreams had vanished.

***

Sala sat in a corner of the dank room. The air reeked of urine mixed with fumes from scattered paint cans and oilcans. Filthy brownish-red streaks stained the walls. No sunshine came in. The only light came from the solitary dim bulb.

Sala sat with his arms behind him. His wrists were bound and they hurt. His back was up against the cold, damp wall. The slightest move made his whole body ache.

The stench of torture hung heavy in the room. Regret washed over him. Why had he allowed Edo to persuade him to come to Jakarta so easily? Markus's kicks and punches had left him weak, inside and out. His heart raced wildly. His eyes pinched shut and fluttered open. His temples throbbed ceaselessly. His whole body was on fire, as though surrounded by flames. He fainted. Oh, how easily happiness could slip away. The visions of Namira and their future together slowly faded.

He had lost track of how long he had been tied up when the door creaked open. The light from outside was bright. A woman came in with a packet of food and a glass of water that she hurriedly put down by the door. A man stood watch over her. He was not Markus. Sala had seen him before at the base. He had a scar on his left cheek.

The man stepped into the room. He untied Sala's hands without a word, and left silently. The woman gave him a last look of pity before the door closed.

Sala stood after he heard the key turn. He walked back and forth to loosen his stiff joints. Was this what it was like to be in jail? But this was worse than a government prison. At least they had beds and the prisoners could see each other, if only to exchange a smile. Here, he was alone.

Sala did not touch the food. He found a rusty nail on the floor and scratched the seven articles of Nevnev on the wall.

Muur nai, suban tai
Never curse or speak ill of another.
Hebang haung
Never do harm to another, whether in
    thought or deed.
Rasung smu-rodang daid
Never harm another through black
    magic or sorcery.
Kef bangil
Never strike another.
Tevh hai sung tavhat
Never stab, cut, or throw things at
    another.
Fedan na, tet wanga
Never kill, maim, or behead another.
Tivak luduk
Never bury alive or drown another.

Sweat poured from his forehead and back. His eyes stung from the concrete dust and paint chips that flew in his face. By the time he was finished, he was drenched in perspiration.

Time kept moving but Sala lost track. Was it night, morning, or afternoon? He felt a stinging pain in his stomach. He looked at the food and could no longer hold out against his hunger. He dug into the rice. A piece of fish that came with it made his tongue itch. His head grew heavy and he felt dizzy. His tongue and face puffed up. He fell unconscious, unable to endure the aching in his head.

Boss Yo came to see him when he was conscious again. He looked like the actor Bucek Depp as he stepped into the room, lit a cigarette, inhaled slowly, and exhaled just as deliberately. His hand flew out, lightning quick, and slapped Sala in the face.

"Do your job or you'll never see this woman again." He showed Sala a photograph of a girl dancing the Sosoy Suar Man-Vuun. A black fan fluttered in her hand. Sala looked at the picture closely. His chest thumped. He knew the girl, the scent of her cheek and the number of moles on her belly.

"Where did you get that photo?" he said.

Boss Yo did not answer.

"Tell me, where did you get that photo?" Sala demanded, but he was the only one who heard the question.

"Don't disobey me. Do your job and one day I'll send you back to Kei. You were the one who chose to come here." Boss Yo turned away as he spoke.

Sala's thoughts were jumbled. He kicked an oilcan at the wall so hard that his toe broke and bled.

Chapter 13

Jakarta, September 2001

On Tuesday night, September 18, the view from the sixth floor of the Hotel Shalira was a riot of colors. Lights bounced off the rain-drenched streets into rainbows. The stuffy, cold night air filled the nine-by-twelve foot room with the reek of death.

From outside the Hotel Shalira did not look inviting, but for the wealthy men of Jakarta it had a special appeal: imported and local women. Manadonese women of mixed Philippine heritage, Sundanese, and those from Taiwan, Thailand, the Ukraine, and Moldova passed through.

A twenty-one-inch television in the room showed special stories about the aftermath of the World Trade Center attacks in New York. Images showed the debris, dirt, and dead bodies being scooped up. A report on strange occurrences the day before the towers were reduced to rubble mentioned a group of top American officials postponing their flight, and Donald Rumsfeld announced that the Pentagon could not account for a missing $2.3 trillion.

Above the bed hung a gold-framed painting of a woman in a revealing white dress like a sari that exposed breasts the size of apples. Her lips seemed to taunt Sala. He tore the painting from the wall and threw it to the floor.

Cold sweat beaded on his face. His chest would not stop thumping. A large man lay prone on the black bed sheets, blood staining his chest. Sala stood over him and checked his pulse. There was none.

The dead man's name was Abraham. It was a beautiful name, a sacred name from the Bible. But this Abraham had met an unfortunate end. Five years earlier, he had taken out a bank loan to start a wheat farm in Pasuruan on the slopes of Mount Bromo. The money was used instead to grow marijuana in Aceh. Five months ago, the police raided the farm and dozens of officers uprooted the growing plants.

Abraham had no way to pay off the loan, and the bank sent five warning letters to his house. He also received threatening phone calls.

At the Hotel Shalira, Abraham had another name. The Manadonese-Filipina girls called him Uncle Baim.

Abraham was still fit at the age of fifty-one. He stood five feet and eight inches tall, smiled a lot, and had a broad forehead and wide nose. He was educated in Singapore. Whenever he went to the Hotel Shalira, he felt like a king ascending his throne. All the girls wanted him.

A little earlier Sala was gripped by doubt. But Edo told him that Boss Yo never made idle threats.

Sala had trouble breathing. I have come this far I may as well complete the job and leave right away, he thought.

With the first stab of the dagger into Abraham's body, Sala's hand shook. "Have mercy, give me a chance," Abraham said, his voice fading. Sala had no choice but to go through with it. Abraham's pleas for mercy faded to a whisper, and collapsed into silence. Sala began weeping. He thought of the bloodshed in the conflict on Kei.

He heard Martina's words echo in his ear: "A real man is one who gets angry only when a woman's honor is sullied. A real man does not fight or spill blood for no good reason."

Sala leaned against the wall and slumped to the floor. Images flitted before his eyes of the dungeon, Boss Yo, and the man with a scar on his left cheek. The last image was of Namira's face, full of acceptance when they became one in the stillness of the Langgur night.

He would have remained mired in regret if not for the cellphone ringing in his pocket. The screen showed Boss Yo's name.

"Is it done?" Boss Yo asked. Sala did not answer, but Boss Yo knew that he had killed Abraham.

"Get rid of your tracks," he said.

"Yeah," Sala shut the phone. He went to the bathroom, peeled off his rubber gloves, and put them into a black plastic bag. He looked at his reflection in the mirror. It was as though he was looking at someone else. The face had red eyes and lips that turned into a snarl to expose the canine teeth. Blood drops stained the corner of the mouth. Sala moved away from the reflection. He rubbed his face. With shaking hands, he turned on the tap. The water poured out at full force. Sala gathered water in his cupped hands to clean himself and the blade of the dagger. The water in the sink turned red before swirling down the drain.

He tried to steady his steps and compose his expression as much as possible as he walked down the corridor lined with rooms on either side. The sound of moans and laughter from one of the rooms made him sick. He threw up in a garbage can near the elevator. Minutes later he disappeared into the dark night.

***

Markus and the man with the scar on his face were waiting in the hotel's basement. They took Sala to a Toyota. His hands felt cold and the thumping in his chest had yet to stop.

He tried to calm his nerves as they drove. He told himself that someone who is happy does not look back or forward. A happy person lives only for today. If I die today because of the sin I have committed, I must fully accept that fate, he thought.

Beside him, Markus gave Boss Yo the news. "The target's been terminated," he said, looking at Sala's ashen face.

Bright fluorescent lights blinded Sala through the car's windows. He was exhausted from grappling with his conscience. Early morning air whistled through a gap in the window, caressing his face.

The universe had proven to be whimsical when it came to a person's journey through life. Sala, who hated the sight of blood being spilled, had just shed someone else's blood.

Snatches of the song that he sang as a child suddenly rang in his ears:

> *Eli went for a walk and found one cent*
> *Eli survived, went to the president's school*
> *Mama hit Eli*
> *It is okay to die*
> *Just as long as you have set foot in Jakarta.*

Chapter 14

Makassar, September 2001

Nana suggested Namira write a letter to Mery. "Your friend might be home," she said on a cold evening.

Namira sat on the cashier's stool and blew into her hands. It had rained incessantly in Makassar, and people stayed indoors. The store did not have any traffic all day. No one had come in, not even to browse or ask the price of an item. Nana knew some of the strangest things, something she had inherited from her husband. She said the ancient Egyptians believed that letters connected the living and the dead. That was why they wrote so much. They wrote on china, linen, and papyrus, and buried the writing with their dead.

"How long has it been since you have heard from her?" Nana asked.

"I left Kei in June, two years ago. I haven't seen or heard any news about my island since then. The reports on television never say anything about Southeast Maluku, they only talk about Ambon," Namira said in despair.

"Send a letter to your friend. I'm sure she is doing fine back there."

Namira nodded. She was touched by the kindness of Nana and Kumala. The two women had taken her in like a member of their family. Sometimes when Nana came home from shopping, she would bring back moisturizing cream, face powder, sanitary pads, and shampoo for Namira.

Nana was reading an article in a magazine about a woman in East Sumba who was the only teacher in a remote village. She taught while carrying her child. Namira took a seat next to Nana. She wanted to speak, but hesitated until Nana asked, "Are you sleepy?"

"Not yet. Actually, I wanted to ask you something but I'm afraid you might be angry."

Nana smiled gently. "Just tell me. You know I think of you as my own daughter."

"I want you to stop paying me for watching the store. The room and board you give me is already more than enough. I just..." Namira trailed off.

"Just what?" Nana saw the hesitation in Namira's face.

"If I want to return home later, would you lend me money? Of course I promise to pay it back."

"There's no need, Namira. I'll keep paying you. You are entitled to receive payment for your work. As for the money to go home, don't worry. I'm glad you are here. It gives Kumala a friend she can talk to. She's happier because she has someone to share things with." Nana paused before continuing, "Ever since her father died she has kept herself occupied with music, books, and drawing. She really misses her father." Nana eyes were filled with sadness.

Namira clasped Nana's hand. "I love Kumala. I think of her as my own sister."

Namira and Nana embraced. Namira knew that behind Nana's smiling face, her beauty, and eye-catching appearance, she hid a deep sorrow, a loneliness born from loyalty. She had snuffed the flames of love the moment her husband's grave was filled in.

Memories of her past with him still came back to her from time to time. After all, people always looked to the past for traces of happiness, for the better times.

Namira saw in Nana a bit of herself. Sala filled her mind. From the moment she came to her senses on board the ship, like Nana she had vowed she would wait for only one man. The man who had made her heart beat faster at Langgur, the man who had made her feel lonely even when he was gone for only two days.

Namira said his name aloud. "Sala."

"*Salah*?" asked Nana, salah being the Indonesian word for "wrong."

"I shouldn't have left Kei without telling my best friend."

Nana smiled and looked away.

Namira could not understand why lately her thoughts turned to Sala. "Is he alright?" she wondered. She got up from the stool and went to the bathroom to look at her reflection in the mirror. Namira breathed on the glass, misting it, and traced the letter S with her finger.

***

Namira finally wrote to Mery. She told her how she was doing and wrote about Kumala, Nana, and the Keumala Store. Mery's reply arrived two months later. She wrote about the reconstruction process in Kei; the clinics and mosques and homes that had been burned down were now being rebuilt.

Namira,

I keep praying that you are well. I was surprised when your letter arrived. After the turmoil in Evu died down, Sala, the boy who often occupied your mind, came looking for you. He went crazy when he couldn't find you. People said he asked everywhere.

Namira, I truly miss you.

A month after we made the peace offering to the people who attacked Evu, volunteers arranged for us to carry out the Vehe Belan. The Warwut people came to Evu, and the Evu people formed a line to Warwut. Mother was emotional the whole journey. I was with the other Evu youths, dancing at the front line. I wore the same kebaya I wore when we danced the Sosoy Swar Man-Vuun.

Beneath the shade of the yellow palm fronds, I saw the men rowing with peaceful faces. Oh Namira, I will never say this enough: I miss you.

> *Come back to Evu. Here is a small map*
> *for you.*
> *Mery K.*

Namira turned the map over. On the back Mery had written, "Carry this in case you have forgotten the way home."

"What did your friend say? Why do you look so sad?" Nana asked when she saw Namira sitting at the cashier's desk with Mery's letter lying on the table before her.

Namira tried to conceal her sadness. "She wrote about the Vehe Belan over there."

"What's that?" Nana asked.

"It's our ritual to end conflict between two villages. The people of both villages visit each other in a line and move like they are rowing a boat."

"Really? Why the rowing motion?" Nana seemed eager for an explanation.

"For the people of Kei, rowing a boat signifies making an effort to reach a destination."

"Tell me more," Nana said eagerly. She was always interested in local cultures. This was reflected in how she dressed: a skirt from Flores cloth, a top made of Lurik batik, wooden bracelets from Bali, and silver earrings from Buton.

"In the line, the womenfolk send their 'children' to relatives in the other village. Behind the women is another line for the men. 'Belan' means boat, and in the Kei tradition this signifies the woman. So 'belan' is a woman giving birth to mankind," Namira said as Nana listened with rapt attention.

"Your birthplace sounds very interesting," she said. "But now you must rest a while."

Namira went to the house for lunch, and Nana watched the store until the afternoon, when Kumala took over. At night, they tended the store together. Nana always chose the afternoon shift because she did not want to take a siesta.

"She is scared she will get fat if she sleeps in the afternoon," Kumala told Namira.

Chapter 15

Boss Yo's base was in a packed and neglected area of North Jakarta. With its tall and rusty iron perimeter fence, the building looked like an abandoned museum. The smell of yeast from a nearby bread factory and clouds of black smoke from the industrial chimneys generated a strange odor in the area.

Sala woke up at five-thirty. His head felt heavy. He got up from his bed and went to the kitchen, where he made a cup of coffee and shook a cigarette from its pack. From his second-floor room window, he saw a boy slide a newspaper through the bars of the gate. He went down and took the newspaper to his room. Abraham's death had made the front page.

Abraham Killed at Shalira
Jakarta. The businessman Abraham, 51, was
found dead with three stab wounds at the Hotel
Shalira on Saturday. He had been stabbed twice
in the chest and once in the abdomen. Rick,
27, the manager of the Hotel Shalira, said the
hotel staff was unable to identify any visitors
Abraham had that night, because unknown
parties had damaged the CCTV camera outside
the elevator leading to Abraham's room.
Jakarta Police Chief Dadang said an
investigation was under way, and he vowed
to solve the case. A manhunt is on for the
perpetrator.

Sala looked at the photo of Abraham's body surrounded by yellow tape. He tore the page from the newspaper and burned it over an ashtray, letting the ashes fall into the hollow. Sala tried to calm his thoughts. He heard a knocking on his door and got up. Edo stood in the doorway.

"Boss Yo wants to see you."

Sala and Edo went down one flight of stairs. They found him, hair coiffed and perfumed, sitting with a cup of coffee.

"This is for you." He tossed a brown envelope on the glass-topped table.

"What is it?" asked Sala.

"Money. You can buy expensive clothes and women."

Sala picked up the envelope and looked inside. It was stuffed with one hundred thousand rupiah notes, held together with a rubber band. Boss Yo was paying him for the killing.

He threw the envelope back on the table. "I don't want expensive clothes or other girls," he said as he turned and left.

Markus moved to stop him, but Boss Yo waved him off. He liked Sala's character. This was someone who did not let money get to his head.

When Sala returned to his room, he tried to think of how to get out. He no longer wanted to stay in Jakarta. There was no one here he knew except for Edo, and asking him for help was the same as swimming into the shark's cage for a second time.

His mind raced as he lay on his wooden bed and considered different plans to escape from the trap he was in. He wanted to return to Kei before December so he could celebrate Christmas there. He wanted to decorate a Christmas tree with lights and play music with Max at the church.

He fell asleep with his mind still racing. He dreamed of a tall, large man, his body covered in hair, dragging him into a cave and tearing off his limbs.

He woke in the late afternoon. The thump of disco music from the next room hurt his head. He went to the bathroom, doused his head with water, and slammed his fist into the wall.

Chapter 16

Namira woke on the night of September 18 with her forehead drenched in a cold sweat. She had dreamed of Sala. He was surrounded by men with spears and powerless to do anything except cover his head with his arms.

The people of her village said that when someone had a nightmare, they should wake up and wash their mouth out three times to prevent the nightmare from becoming real. Namira went to the sink, leaned over, and opened her mouth beneath the tap. She rinsed out her mouth three times, but could not go back to sleep. She went to the living room where Nana had left her magazine, and began reading.

***

The hour hand on the clock touched nine when Namira came out of the bathroom. She kept asking herself why her thoughts lately were so preoccupied with Sala, culminating in the nightmare the previous night. When she arrived at the store, she dusted the sideboard and the piano.

Nana looked beautiful every day. She said a storekeeper had to keep up appearances so that people would keep coming to the store.

"Give them something easy on the eyes," she said. This morning Nana wore a long cockle-brown dress. Her headscarf was peanut butter brown. Namira got up on a stepladder and dusted the rooster lamp. She also cleaned the dust clinging to the glass of the old map and the wayang painting. Both women were busy when the phone next to the cashier's desk rang. Namira answered it.

"Hello, good morning." She knew the voice very well.

"Mery?" Namira squealed in delight.

"You still recognize my voice. How are you?"

Namira's eyes misted as she listened to Mery. "I'm good. How are you? Are Uncle Pieter and Aunt Emili doing well?"

"My parents are fine and healthy. They've been worried about you this whole time."

"I really miss them." Namira's voice cracked with emotion. She looked at Nana, who smiled.

"Go ahead. Let me finish the cleaning," Nana said.

"You're terrible, Ra. You should have let someone know you were leaving," Mery said.

"It wasn't like that, Mer. You know how I always freeze when things get crazy. I was pulled away, and the next thing I knew I was on a ship."

Mery was silent for a moment.

"When will you come back to Kei? I'm in Yogyakarta, Ra. Mother wants me to enroll at the university here."

"You're in Yogyakarta?"

"Yes. Mother forwarded your letter to me. That's why it took so long for me to reply. I want to see you when I'm in Kei for Christmas. Come home too and we'll meet there."

"Okay, Mer," Namira said happily.

"Kei needs you," Mery said just before she hung up.

Chapter 17

Sala was sick of Markus and Boss Yo. He had heard that some of Boss Yo's men were involved in the violence in Ambon.

Markus came looking for him. "Boss Yo wants to see you."

Sala went down, barely concealing his annoyance. Every time he left the base, he wore a black cap or hooded jacket to hide his face. He worried about meeting anyone who might recognize him from Hotel Shalira.

"There's no need to be scared. Jakarta is a jungle. No one pays attention to you," Edo told him.

Sala had kept to himself since the killing of Abraham. When he was asked anything, he responded with just one or two words. He wore a permanent expression of sadness. No one saw him happy. At the base, the only person he spoke to was Ali, a ten-year-old boy. Ali's job was to clean, make coffee, and buy cigarettes. Sometimes he was sent to the market to buy food.

Ali's parents were distant relatives of Boss Yo from the village of Faan, on the east coast of Kei Kecil. They had died in the fire when their home was burned down. Ali had stayed at a friend's house until Boss Yo brought him to the base. The boy loved talking with Sala. He told Sala about how he was better than the other kids in his village at spinning a top, a girl back home who was crazy about him, and how he missed eating banana blossoms with lime hot sauce.

He knocked on Sala's door in the middle of the night when his tooth hurt. Most of his teeth were brown and full of cavities. Sala prepared a glass of salt water and told Ali to swish the solution in his mouth. When the base was empty, Ali asked Sala to teach him to play the guitar.

Thursday afternoon all the men at the base headed off to Bogor, leaving behind only the Flores hit man who worked for Boss Yo. Sleep was alien to him. He stood watch over the base while Boss Yo took the others out for a bit of recreation. Sala and Ali did not want to go along.

After they were done eating lunch together, Ali asked Sala, "Are you a killer like Uncle Yo, Uncle Markus, and Uncle Edo?"

"Do I look like a bad person?" Sala asked back.

Ali looked at him for a moment and smiled. "You look like a movie star."

Sala looked at Ali with a blank stare.

To Ali, Sala was different from the other men at the base. His face looked much kinder. Sala was also quieter and did not boss him around. While the other men ordered him to make coffee and buy cigarettes for them, or sanitary pads for their wives and girlfriends, Sala did everything himself.

Ali enjoyed sleeping with Sala because it gave him the chance to ask all kinds of questions.

"Why don't you ask me to make coffee? Is mine no good?"

"I don't want to bother you."

Ali fell silent on hearing Sala's response. He asked, "Why do you always look so sad?"

"That's just how I am."

"Do you have a girlfriend?"

Sala's expression went dreamy at that question.

"You do," Ali pressed on.

Sala nodded. He did not know if Namira had someone else by now, but he felt they were still together. He was sure they would meet again.

"What's her name? Is she beautiful? Where is she now?"

Sala did not answer.

"Did you have a fight?"

Sala still did not answer.

"Why not just marry her?"

"Ali, if you ask one more question, you can sleep by yourself. I'll go to another room."

His threat silenced Ali.

When Sala woke the next morning, Ali was no longer next to him. He found a cup of coffee, a cigarette, and a note: "I hope the coffee and cigarette help you stop being sad. I'm sorry it's just one cigarette. I stole it from Uncle Flores. Please don't be mad about all the questions I asked last night."

When he read the note, Sala smiled.

***

Sala met with Boss Yo. The man had another assignment for him. Sala was disgusted at the prospect.

"You need to train harder in martial arts. At the end of November I want you to go to Balikpapan."

"I won't do anything," Sala spat back. He was the only one who did not call Yohanes Boss Yo.

"Then you'll find the corpse of this young lady, Namira."

"Where is she? Where are you hiding her?" Sala roared.

Markus grabbed him and pinned his arms behind his back.

"Do your job in Balikpapan. After that, Markus will tell you," Boss Yo said.

Sala was powerless each time they threatened Namira.

After Sala left the room, Markus, Boss Yo, and Edo doubled over with laughter. They did not know the whereabouts of the girl with the fan. All they knew was her name and that she was Sala's girlfriend in Kei. Edo had taken the picture of her at the Tutup Sasi Laut in Elaar.

"You're really smart." Boss Yo slapped Edo on the back.

Edo liked being praised by Boss Yo. It meant a hefty bonus at the end of the year.

***

Sala had terrible visions: a man with bulging eyes, a bullet nestled in a chest, an arrow piercing a heart, a scythe cutting through an artery, and a dagger repeatedly stabbing someone in the back.

His waking moments were filled with gruesome images of body parts, and he was the one doing the mutilating in every scene. He remembered a Buddhist verse, "We are what we think. All that we are arises with our thoughts. With our thoughts, we make the world. Speak or act with an impure mind and trouble will follow you, as the wheel follows the ox that draws the cart." Sala tried to banish all thoughts of murder from his mind.

He was determined to leave the base, perhaps not today or next week, but one day. He definitely would be free.

Chapter 18

Balikpapan, November 2001

Sala found Boss Yo sitting with a woman wearing fire-red lipstick. She reminded Sala of the girl who loved roller-skating in the movie, *Lupus*.

"You have to go to Balikpapan for an important job. When you get back to Jakarta, I'll introduce you to a beautiful woman."

Sala remained quiet. He did not like the sound of this.

Boss Yo handed him a photograph of a man with a low forehead and a nose that sat flat on his face. He had a mole above his eyebrow. "This man deserves to be killed. He runs an illegal logging operation, and a nickel mining company in Central Sulawesi. The company exploited one of the villages in the area, flooding it and muddying its rivers."

Boss Yo knew Sala would never refuse an order as long as he threatened Namira, and would be willing to kill if he thought the target was a criminal who had hurt others.

He liked how Sala had carried out his first hit. He was nervous and doubtful, but cold and disciplined. He had not made any small talk with the target, or approached him by offering a drink, phoning him, or engaging in some other undercover act. Sala had gotten straight to the point. Boss Yo's other men often needed weeks, sometimes months, of undercover work and tailing a target before getting down to business.

When Sala killed the first time, he shivered at the sight of blood spurting from Abraham. The blood reminded him of his mother's death and of the conflict in Kei.

But to Boss Yo, Sala was simply skilled at what he did.

***

Sala stayed at the Hotel Gerindra in Balikpapan Permai area. He liked the hotel. It was close to the shops, bus terminal, and the beach. The thermostat in his room was set at sixty-six degrees.

He wanted to calm his mind by resting all day. Perhaps he would listen to instrumental music while thinking of ways to kill the illegal logger and erase every trace of himself.

The logger often went to the Limaru Pub on Thursday nights. Sala would kill him there. He drew up a plan. He might not even need a weapon.

He checked his dagger, a gift from a friend in Makassar. He had used it to save someone from an attack by the Legos gang in Blok M. The presence of gangs in Blok M could be traced back to the proliferation of gangs throughout Jakarta in the 1960s. The gang in Blok M had always been known as Legos because they started out selling *melego*, goods at the flea market at Taman Puring. Most of their members came from Surabaya.

Sala wiped the dagger with a damp towel. He looked down at the empty, wet street through the large window.

Every time I'm on a job the weather gets like this, he thought. It was as though the night could sense that a death was being planned. Sala scratched his head, and flakes of dandruff floated down. He had not washed his hair in three days.

He went into the bathroom and soaked his hair before washing it with the hotel shampoo that was neither foamy nor scented. He dried his hair with a towel as he came out of the bathroom, and lay down on the bed with a magazine.

He flipped the pages to an article about the sexual behavior of monogamous animals. Owls and penguins were the birds most loyal to their mates, or so the article stated.

Sala thought of his mother. She had never married after the man she loved abandoned her. A few times a customer at her metal workshop proposed, but she had remained unmoved. When Sala asked her why she refused to marry, she said, "We're all created with one partner, one man for one woman. To take more would be greedy."

Sala also remained loyal to one partner, a woman whose whereabouts he did not know. Namira had locked the door to his heart, and the key was tossed into the ocean.

How I miss the smell of her cheek.

The faces of Martina and Namira danced in his thoughts.

When he was younger, Sala had a classmate, Frins, whose father worked at the local government office. Frins had mocked him when he brought steamed enbal for lunch.

"How pitiful, eating enbal all the time. My father says that cassava make the brain stop working. How can you be smart when you only eat food that comes out of the ground? Look what I brought, rice and instant noodles."

He punched Frins in the face and went home before class was over. At home, he pouted, "From now on, I won't eat cassava and sago. I want instant noodles and rice."

Martina became angry. She looked Sala in the eye and said, "I made the enbal and sago myself. I made it for you."

"But I've never eaten rice."

"Just eat enbal," Martina barked.

He cried and only when he was older, he understood that his mother wanted to maintain the local tradition.

***

Balikpapan in the morning was like any other coastal town, with the smell of the sea and the searing heat of the sun. Sala did not like having breakfast in the hotel restaurant and eating in front of so many people, even if no one paid any attention to him.

Before it became famous as an oil town, Balikpapan was a fishing village. The folk tales told by those who grew up there spoke of a king who threw his daughter into the sea to protect her from his enemies. She was set adrift on a raft of planks, or *papan*, tied together. When a wave struck the raft, it overturned, *terbalik*. A fisherman found the princess, and the place was named Balikpapan.

Sala tucked stray strands of hair under his cap. He planned to go to a supermarket in the morning to buy toiletries and socks. Boss Yo had phoned him earlier, ordering him to finish the job as soon as possible and return to Jakarta.

***

Bre kissed his wife on the cheek as she stood in the doorway. He wore a suit, carried a briefcase, and left for the office. Bre and a partner from Japan met later that night at the Limaru Pub, to talk about a possible venture in the timber business. Bre loved timber and pubs. The Limaru was his favorite. He went there whenever his wife, who ran a clothing boutique, went shopping in Singapore.

Inside the pub, the night smelled of alcohol and perfume, and dazzling lights showed off the ethnic décor.

Bre sat in a corner talking with a man wearing glasses. They occasionally took sips from glasses of Chivas Regal. Bre was an illegal logger who could not be touched by the police. He was a shadow to them. Even if his operation was discovered, the police only arrested the truck drivers and barge operators transporting the logs. Bre had many tentacles.

In his house, both servants were sound asleep and Sala waited for him in the dark. Bre would die at his hands. The next day, his death made the headlines in the *Kaltim Tribun, Kaltim Post, Balikpapan Pos, Koran Kaltim,* and *Sapos.*

169

***

Sala had just finished a glass of orange juice and a boiled egg when a news report appeared on the TV in his room. Thirty-one-year-old Abdul Malik had slept with a thirteen-year-old babysitter who lived in an alley in Ambon.

Abdul was a *sharia* enforcer of an Islamic organization. His peers offered him two choices: punishment by stoning, so that God would have mercy on him, or if he refused the stoning, he would have to answer to God. Abdul chose the stoning. He had signed a statement confessing to adultery. The stoning was shown live on television.

As the midday shadows crept across downtown Ambon, Abdul lowered himself into a hole in the ground surrounded by men dressed in white tunics. Dirt was shoveled in, burying him up to his chest. A heap of stones lay before the sharia enforcers.

"Did you truly commit adultery as described?" their commander asked.

"Yes."

"Are you willing to go through with this stoning?"

"*Insha'Allah*, I am willing."

The commander appeared sad, but joined the row of other enforcers. Stones flew at Abdul's head. Blood spurted from his wounds and rocks covered his head. People in the watching crowd cried. Sala felt sick. He staggered to the bathroom and vomited.

His head was in an uproar. He had killed two people who were considered sinners. He had agreed to the murders of Abraham and Bre. He had agreed to commit murder if the proposed target was a criminal. Sala held his head in his hands as he slumped to the cold floor.

Chapter 19

Nana and Kumala said goodbye to Namira at the seaport of Makassar. The night before, Nana had made buns studded with citron and raisins for the girl. She also gave her an envelope holding six hundred thousand rupiah.

"This is for meals along the way," she said as she held Namira tight.

"It's so hard for us to let you go," Nana blurted.

"I'm so sad to have to leave you and Kumala." Namira's eyes moistened.

"If you ever come to Makassar again, please call us," Kumala said.

"Yes. You're my family here."

The ship's horn blew. An announcement came over the loudspeaker; the ship would set sail in ten minutes.

Kumala took a piece of paper out of her bag. It was a sketch of Namira.

"Is this a farewell gift?" Namira asked.

"No, a friendship gift. Have a safe trip," Kumala said.

Namira grasped Nana's hand and kissed it. Then she embraced Kumala. She hated ports at times like this. She let go of Kumala and headed to the crowd of passengers, unable to look back.

Nana and Kumala watched Namira disappear in the crowd. Everyone seemed in a hurry to board the ship.

The *Bukit Siguntang* cast off and slowly moved from the dock.

It was hot on the ship. The smell of sweat rose like the scent of acacia early in the morning. To the left and right, front and back, people slept along the length of the deck. Little children cried from the heat.

Namira asked the elderly man next to her to keep an eye on her suitcase. She wanted to get some air on level seven, where the café sold fruit juice. What she enjoyed about travel by ship was that people were always willing to help one another.

***

The café was deserted. Only three people were inside, sitting far from each other. An effeminate man brought her a menu. He also sold imported cigarettes and fake Rolex watches. Namira ordered a glass of apple juice. Apples were good for seasickness. Whenever Namira and Mery traveled between islands, Emiliana made sure they packed an apple.

She sipped her juice as she looked over the expanse of ocean. The smell of the sea was strong. She thought of Kei.

It had stayed in her vision. Being on the sea made Namira feel alone, like she was the only person left in the universe. She was gripped by sorrow and thought of her mother. A year had passed since had she heard anything of her. She did not even know if her mother was still alive. Her vision misting over, she began weeping.

Mother, where are you? Are you happy? Are you looking at me? I miss you. I miss your cooking. I miss your scolding. I miss looking at you sitting at your sewing machine for hours. Mother, I miss the little things the most.

She had almost finished the juice when a large man with a stump where his left hand should have been approached her. He wore a red shirt and had a tattoo, and took the seat across from her. She looked at his jawline, eyes, nose, and lips. Namira could tell they both came from the same place.

"Pardon me for sitting here. I'm Roni, but you can call me Ron."

Namira nodded warily.

He regarded her closely. "From Maluku?"

Namira shuddered. Ron's eyes were scary from the cataract clouding his right eye.

"Me too."

"I knew that. What island are you from?"

"Kei Kecil."

"Where on Kei, Watraan, Langgur, Depur, or Dian?"

"Elaar."

"Do you have time to chat?"

Namira started to be annoyed. A man who looked like him was expected to be quiet. Why was he so chatty?

Looking at Ron was like watching Steven Seagal host a gossip show.

"Well, do you?" he asked again.

Namira nodded.

"Look, I want to go home to Ambon. I lived in Jakarta for five years, working as a debt collector. It was the worst job I have ever had. I was not happy, so I ran away. I want to go home. I miss *Ambon Manise*, but what I really miss are my wife and child. When I left Ambon my wife was pregnant. My child must be four years old now."

"So?" Namira could not take it anymore. Where was Ron going with all this? Why was he pouring out his heart to a stranger?

"A crewmember is selling clothes on level six, and I want to buy some for my wife and kid. But I can't see colors that well. I caught a sliver of glass in my eye during the violence in Ambon. Would you help me choose clothes with the right colors?"

Namira choked. She felt a pang of guilt for thinking badly of him. Negative thoughts always left her with a sense of shame.

"Are you alright?" Ron asked.

"I'm fine, the juice is not very good." Namira went to the cashier, but Ron paid before she could. They walked toward the stairs leading down to level six. People stared at them in surprise. Ron's stump drew a lot of attention.

Namira picked out a sea-blue frock with a picture of a sailfish. She also chose a maroon girl's top with lace across the front, and a skirt with a picture of an umbrella. She described the clothes to Ron.

Ron nodded happily. His intimidating look disappeared with the change of his mood.

"Is that all?" Namira asked.

"Are there other colors that look good to you?"

"There is another pea-green one, and very plain. Do you want it?"

"Sure, get that one too."

Namira picked out another set of children's clothes.

Ron invited her to the restaurant on level five, usually reserved for the ship's VIP passengers. The other patrons stared as they entered.

Namira ordered grilled snapper with hot sauce. Ron ordered goat fried-rice. It was odd how often luck found her in life, even something small like Ron paying for her juice and dinner.

They talked as they ate. Namira become comfortable around Ron. She also felt safe, since everyone must have known Ron was a gangster.

Ron told her about riots and gangs. He confessed that he had been involved in stoking the violence in Ambon and said he was sorry.

"Ambonese gang members in Jakarta were paid to instigate the chaos there. When I remember it now, I want to die."

Namira choked on her food.

Ron continued talking. "It was really tragic. The gangs that helped start the riots forced their fellow Ambonese to flee to the big cities, including Jakarta. Life in the city is hard, so some refugees became gang members too. It's like a circle."

Namira disagreed with him. "Many people who left Ambon have gone on to be successful in government and entertainment."

"That's true," Ron nodded vigorously.

"Speaking of which, why did you say you were involved in the riots?" Namira asked.

"During the riots, the one thousand gang members involved in the Ketapang incident were sent to Ambon. I was among them," Ron said slowly. He had regret in his voice.

Namira swallowed. "Why are you telling me?"

"I thought you were a university student going home for the holidays," Ron said.

She shook her head. "I'm one of the riot victims and I want to go home."

"I want to go home too," Ron said. Perhaps what he really wanted to say was, "I was involved in the violence, and I'm sorry. I want to go home."

"Who paid the gang members to cause trouble in Maluku?" Namira asked, annoyed.

"The devils with the money. The foreign devils."

Ron left his answer at that. Namira wanted to ask more, but suppressed the urge.

They talked in the restaurant for almost four hours. Through the porthole next to their table, Namira saw the sun setting, a ball of fire disappearing into the depths of the ocean. The call to the sunset prayers came over the loudspeaker.

"Are you Muslim?" Ron asked. He grabbed a tissue.

Namira nodded.

"In that case you had better get ready. It is almost *maghrib*. The prayer room is on level seven, toward the back. You know where it is, right?"

"Are you praying?" Namira asked.

Ron shook his head. "I'm Protestant."

Namira said goodbye and Ron thanked her again.

After worship, Namira returned to level four, where she had camped out earlier. She found the elderly man having dinner. He had just received his ration for passengers.

Namira apologized for having left him for so long with her suitcase.

He laughed. "It's nothing, child. That's how it should be on board. I find traveling on ships more humane than flying. In a plane, everyone is caught up with themselves."

Namira smiled. She curled up on the paper cement sack. She was tired. Moments later she was fast asleep.

***

Namira saw her mother in a white dress, riding a white horse, like a woman knight. She smiled and held out her hand. Namira leaped on the back of the horse and sat behind her mother. They rode on the surface of the sea.

"Where are we going, Mother?"

"We're going home, home to Kei, child."

"Why have you waited so long to come for me? Where have you been?"

"I had to pick up your father and show him the road to our new home."

"Will you take me?"

"Not yet. You still have a long time to go."

"But I want to be with you and Father. I miss you," Namira cried.

"Do not be sad, child. Your father and I will protect you from the sky."

The horse slowed and her mother lowered her to an island she did not recognize. Then her mother was gone, sucked into the sky. Namira screamed.

***

Namira woke with her heart racing. She wiped her face and tied her hair back.

The man next to her held out a glass of water. "You were crying in your sleep, child."

"I dreamed about my mother." Namira leaned back against the wall of the ship. She tried to recall the dream. *Oh Mother, are you with Father? Is that the message you are trying to send me?*

A sense of relief flooded Namira's heart after the dream, but she could not say why.

Chapter 20

Namira's return to Kei was filled with relief and joy. No matter how far from home anyone ventured, they always wanted to return to their birthplace. It was a basic human instinct.

The *Bukit Siguntang* docked at Ambon's port. Ron helped Namira with her suitcase. He also accompanied her to buy a ticket to Tual. Ambon was not yet free of the conflict. In the year that Namira was in Makassar, Ambon continued to be rocked by violence. News reports showed:

August 2001: A bomb exploded in Nusawungu, killing four people and injuring seventeen.

A bomb exploded in Mahardika, killing four people and injuring more than a dozen.

October 2001: An armed group attacked the village of Suli, Salahutu. Five people were killed.

November 2001: Reds attacked Whites in a clove orchard. The military joined in the attack against the Whites. Several Muslims were killed.

Namira bought her ferry ticket to Tual as the Iwan Fals song, "*Puing II*," played on the radio.

> *The footprints of the refugees*
> *Mingle with suffering.*
> *The footprints of the refugees*
> *Speak to those in power*
> *About livestock that died*
> *About friends who died*
> *About a brother who died*
> *About a father who died*
> *About a mother who died.*

Namira's breath caught at the last line.

***

She continued her journey by boat to Tual, grateful to be in Kei. From Tual she caught a wooden boat to Evu. Her plan was to go to Elaar after visiting Evu. She wondered what her house would be like after being abandoned for more than a year. Would it still be standing, or would there be nothing left? During the conflict, the Muslims who lived on the coast had fled inland, and escaped into the mountains and the forests.

Throughout her journey to Evu, Namira thought of Mery's family. She remembered the goodness of Emiliana and Pieter. Mery had insisted that she visit them first.

The boat pulled up at the dock at Evu. It was still early, and Namira's body cast a long shadow to the west. She got off the boat and started walking to Mery's house. She wanted to surprise her.

Evu had not changed much. The refugee tents were no longer there, and neither were the posts set up by the foreign and local NGOs. The refugees had returned to their homes.

***

Namira knocked on the carved teak door. The morning was still quiet. A handful of chickens scratched away at the ground in the front yard.

"Good morning," Namira called out. There was no response from inside the house. Namira walked around to Mery's window. It was shut tight. Nothing had changed in the two years she had been gone, except the water-cherry tree outside Mery's window was now laden with fruit.

"Mer," Namira tapped at the window, and heard a muffled voice.

"Mer. I'm here, Namira."

Mery bolted awake. She did not bother fixing her hair before opening the window.

"Oh my God, you should have let me know you were arriving today. Mama, Namira has come." Mery ran to the living room and opened the front door.

Emiliana had been up since dawn, and followed her daughter into the living room. Mery and Namira embraced each other.

"Oh child, where have you been? We worried about you every day." Emiliana's eyes glassed over.

Tears flowed from Namira's eyes. She flung herself into Emiliana's arms and cried.

"I was in Makassar, Auntie. When things went crazy in Evu, I was dragged on the ship."

"I'm just grateful that you are home. Kei is safe. The conflict did not consume Evu. We performed the Vehe Belan."

"I know, Auntie. Mery told me in her letter."

Pieter woke shortly after and joined in welcoming Namira.

Mery took Namira's suitcase and brought her into her room. Emiliana went to the kitchen to make breakfast. At the stroke of eight, they gathered around the dining table.

"It feels like so long since we last ate together." Emiliana set out the bowls of mung bean *kolak*. As they ate, she told Namira how Kei healed from the conflict.

"The tribal elders worked hard to bring peace through a traditional oath. All the people of Kei gathered at the Lodar El field in Tual to take the oath. The ritual to cleanse villages that had fought each other was already carried out in almost all of Kei. Everyone was asked to renounce the violations they committed.

"It was an anomaly. Kei was at peace, but in Ambon the violence raged on." Emiliana paused before adding casually, "Many parties do not want to see Ambon at peace. You can see it in the lack of commitment by the authorities in trying to bring peace to the rival groups."

The reconciliation efforts in Kei had worked, and reconstruction was under way. The damaged homes were being rebuilt, one by one. Public facilities were also being rebuilt.

The seeds of peace in Kei began to spread. No more reports of villages attacking each other. Old grudges disappeared as though sucked into a giant hole. The refugees returned to their homes and old lives. Markets were open and running. The Buginese, Javanese, and Buton traders were back doing business.

"But history will show that two hundred people were killed. Four thousand homes were burned. Thirty thousand people across Kei fled from their homes, and those who went missing died of dysentery, fever, and malaria." Emiliana recited the numbers as though they were a poem. She suddenly lost her appetite to finish breakfast.

"Let's not talk about it. What's important is that we are all safe," Pieter said. Namira looked from Emiliana to Pieter. He knew it hurt his wife to talk about the death toll.

Mery tried to lighten the mood by talking about the oath she took a year ago. "Mama, Papa, and I went to Tual, and Volvot too. He'll be back at work next week." She went on talking about the peace ceremony held in Tual. "Praise be to God, the oath to keep the peace forever was heeded in Kei."

We are all Kei people. We drink from the
same spring and eat from the same land, the
land of Kei. As the tribal king, I vow that if

there is anyone who eats, drinks, and lives from this land but has a dirty heart and desires chaos, then all the filth and disease that have been mixed with water will be their drinking water. And they will eat and bathe with that same water.

All the poison rooted in the ground will be their food and their home. Disease and distress will be their drink and will cover them for all time, everywhere. But for those who live on this land, and keep and protect the Kei land from conflict and chaos, the water of the Kei land will cleanse them and their family of filth and disease. The land will enrich their lives.

That morning, Namira still could not believe she was back, enjoying life in her homeland. She relished every moment. No one was in a hurry like in the big city, and most importantly, Kei was at peace.

Chapter 21

Sala returned to Jakarta the day after he murdered Bre. When he arrived at the base, he went straight to his room and started packing. He had returned for one reason only: to say goodbye to Ali. The boy watched motionless as he emptied his closet.

When Sala was done, he put his hand on Ali's shoulder and whispered, "Be good here. Don't be naughty. These people will not hurt you. Don't get mixed up in other people's business. Mind your own." His eyes burned as he spoke.

Ali was stunned. It was the most Sala had said in all the time they had been together. "Are you leaving?" Ali's expression slowly changed. He looked like he was about to cry. "Why are you leaving?"

"I have something I need to do, something very important."

"Will you look for your girlfriend?"

"You're asking too many questions again."

"I'm losing someone I really like," Ali said.

Sala went to Ali and hugged him. "Learn to be a real man, Ali."

The boy sobbed. He could not hold back his tears.

Sala took his guitar hanging on the wall. "This is for you. Keep practicing until your fingernails break."

Ali was quiet. He took a brown stone from his pocket, and said, "It's a magical stone, a river stone. My late grandfather gave it to me. He said that whoever holds this stone will be invincible. Take it."

Sala shook his head. "No. Your grandfather left it to you, and you should not give it to anyone else." He closed Ali's fingers around the brown rock.

"Go now. I won't rat on you. Only a lowlife rats on others." Ali tried not to break out in tears again and slipped the brown stone into Sala's bag.

Sala hugged him longer the second time. If Ali were not the nephew of Boss Yo, he would have taken the boy with him.

Elsewhere on the base, the men gathered at a table to play cards. Beer bottles were scattered everywhere, and the air was thick with cigarette smoke. Their laughter bounced off the walls. They were half drunk.

Two women had passed out with their faces flat on the table. The smell of alcohol and nicotine permeated the air in the room. Markus, who had been losing, took his girlfriend by the hand to his room.

"He can't hold it any longer," the Flores man taunted him.

Markus did not care.

Sala crept downstairs, stepping carefully, his body pressed against the wall. He held the dagger in his hand. He was already thinking ahead. If anyone tried to stop him, he would not hesitate to take action. His heart thumped with each stair.

He moved as softly as possible. When he set foot on the final step, he breathed a sigh of relief. He turned and hid behind the stairs before heading for the back door. Just as he reached for the doorknob, a loud banging came from the main door of the base. A voice over a loudspeaker ordered everyone to stay where they were. The police had come.

"The building is surrounded. Do not try to resist."

Sala's heart was racing. With one kick, he was out the back door. His chest thumped harder and his adrenaline surged. He scaled a fence and landed in a narrow, deserted alley. He emerged on a football field surrounded by high walls covered with graffiti.

A police officer saw him run from the building and fired a warning shot into the air. "Freeze!" he yelled.

Sala did not look back, or stop. His feet flew over the muddy ground.

"Freeze! Police!"

Sala's instinct told him to run as fast as he could.

Am I a sadistic criminal to this enforcer of the law? They should forgive me. I never ordered children to slay their own parents. I'm not someone who goes against God and kills thousands of people. I only killed two people who had made others miserable. Was I wrong? Of course, I was wrong. Taking their lives should never have been my job, but they should see it as God striking them down through me.

Sala saw a supermarket ahead of him and ran inside. Everyone turned to watch. Sala crashed into a woman pushing a cart. He looked behind but did not see the policeman. He ran out of the supermarket and climbed the stairs to an overhead footbridge.

The policeman caught up with him. A struggle broke out on the footbridge.

Sala twisted the officer's arm behind his back, grabbed his revolver, and kicked it away. The policeman was no less agile, as he was trained to fight people like Sala. He grabbed the knife tucked inside Sala's belt and stabbed him in the abdomen. Blood spurted, reddening his clothes.

The crowd gathered below the bridge looked at each other, then back at Sala and the policeman. As the blood dripped from Sala's body and he fell to the asphalt below, women in the crowd screamed.

Sala closed his eyes and saw Abraham's sprawled body and Bre lying face down, and the bodies of the victims of violence in Kei.

"God, I truly need a miracle," Sala muttered. He was almost out of breath, but managed to stand and throw himself at the officer. The officer fell and Sala took the chance to run, pressing the gash on his stomach. He saw stars before his vision blurred. His steps began to falter and a thought crossed his mind: my life is no longer mine.

A car careened toward him from behind and pulled up. Edo opened the door and dragged Sala inside. The siren of a police car grew louder, but it was stuck in Jakarta traffic. Edo's arrival was a miracle.

Edo left Sala with two of his associates, Stepen and Obet, crewmembers aboard the *Bukit Siguntang*. Stepen hid Sala in a cabin stacked with crates of cuttlefish. He opened Sala's shirt and pressed a bandage to his wound.

Squinting, Sala saw regret on Edo's face.

"I can't stay long, pela. Take care of yourself. I'll try to divert the police's attention. I pray for the day we meet again. Forgive me," Edo said.

It came to him in a jumble, but Sala still heard the words.

Edo took off Sala's cap and shirt. "Put this on, Obet. You owe me for saving your life. It's payback time," Edo said hurriedly.

A gang had beaten Obet for going out with the girlfriend of a Makassarese gangster. The man was not pleased, and gathered his men to wait for the *Bukit Siguntang* to dock. When the other passengers had disembarked, they dragged Obet on the deck and threw him overboard to the concrete pier. They took him into a warehouse full of oil drums and rusted iron and tortured the twenty-five-year-old.

Obet did not have it in him to fight back. One against ten gave no chance for someone without knowledge of any kind of self-defense. His lip was split and bleeding. He was clubbed and kicked repeatedly. Fortunately, Edo and his men arrived. A huge brawl erupted between the two gangs.

Obet put on Sala's bloodstained shirt and cap without a word.

"Get in the car. We need to get away from here."

Edo and Obet sped away from the port. The police, late on the scene, took Obet for Sala and followed the car. Edo was trained by Boss Yo to drive like a racecar driver, and weaved through crowded streets.

***

The ship's horn blew for the third time and the gangplank and anchor were raised. The *Bukit Siguntang* set off from the port of Tanjung Priok. A long time ago, Tanjung Priok was not full of sin, or filthy, or flooded, or fogged with pollution like now. Tanjung Priok in the time of the Dutch colonial government was a clean port free of floods. Boats from the yacht club moored along the pier.

From the porthole of the cabin, the fluorescent lights of the shore dwindled. Sala held his stomach. His fingers were drenched in blood. He opened his rucksack and fumbled for a bandage. He felt something hard and pulled it out. In his hand was Ali's brown river stone. He smiled and mumbled, "That darn stubborn little kid."

The ship was headed to Buton, Makassar, and Ambon. Oh, the pain. If he could negotiate with the angel of death, Sala wanted to take his last breath on the Banda Sea.

Sala's face was pale from blood loss. He wanted to write a letter—this could be the last he saw of life. He rummaged in his bag and found a pen but not any paper. He dug deeper, using the strength he had left. He found a pack of cigarettes. He tore it into a rectangle of sorts, and wrote with trembling fingers.

Namira,

My life is probably at its end. The only thing I want now is to see your face, to feel your fingers again, and inhale the smell of your cheek. I haven't made anything of myself here. The goodness inside me has truly gone away. I've been trapped by my own actions. Murder, sadness, perversity, and regret have no meaning. Jakarta has no goodness at all. It would never suit your gentle heart.

Two lives have been lost because of me, but can I call that fate? Which angel will come for me? Will I be granted wings on the other side, or become food for maggots beneath the ground? I truly regret immersing myself in the darkness.

Ah, death truly is near.
I love you. Until death.
With the same love as always,
Sala
P.S.: My love, if I am gone and we never meet again, I bequeath to you the porcelain tea set buried beneath the shade of the noni tree at my house in Watraan.

Sala's hand shook. His vision grew hazy. The pen slipped from his hand and fell to the floor. He folded the cigarette pack and put it back into his bag. He doubted the letter would find its way to Namira. He knew the angel of death would come for him before he had finished the journey home. His vision grew darker and darker, until his eyes closed.

Even if it is here, at least every breath of air tastes of the sea.

***

Eighteen hundred miles from the Java Sea, Namira was fast asleep in a wooden house on the beach. She shivered as she dreamed of wet, white sand. The waves lapped at the shore. She sat on the carpet of sand, holding Sala's head in her lap.

"Stroke my head," Sala said.

She did, caressing his scalp until a wave crashed into them.

Namira woke up, her forehead slick with sweat. It was a strange dream, a message from a distant sea. A sign.

Her heart pounded in her chest. She hugged her pillow tight and murmured, "Come home, my love. We don't have to be alone when we are old. Come to me, I miss you so much."

Notes

Chapter 1

Enbal: Food staple made from fermented cassava, the main food crop in Southeast Maluku.

Roro: *Bunga roro*, a tuberose known in Indonesian as *sedap malam*.

Jilbab: Indonesian for *hijab*, the headscarf covering the neck and hair of Muslim women.

Chapter 2

Sosoy Swar Man-Vuun: A dance performed to honor guests.

Kebaya: Traditional combination blouse and dress worn by Indonesian women.

Tutup Sasi Laut: A traditional resource management system with set opening and closing seasons. Closing the marine sasi means ending fishing and collecting of marine resources, especially sea cucumber and mother of pearl shells.

Tifa drums: Hourglass-shaped drum made of wood and stretched lizard skin.

Pak: Respectful term of address for an older man, meaning "father."

Eid al-Adha: Muslim "Feast of the Sacrifice," marking the end of the annual Hajj pilgrimage to Mecca.

Kecubung: Perennial herb with large, trumpet-shaped flowers, also known as *Datura metel*.

"…monetary crisis breaking out…": Beginning in 1997, the rupiah dropped from 2600 to 11,000 rupiah to the US dollar. A rescue package of $23 billion from the International Monetary Fund was unable to stabilize the currency and inflation continued to rise.

Chapter 3

"*Olesio sayange…*": "Rasa Sayange," a popular folk song from the Malukus.

Kasbi bread: Bread made from cassava flour.

President B.J. Habibie: Bacharuddin Jusuf Habibie, appointed vice president by President Suharto in 1998 and became president after Suharto's resignation.

Noni tree: *Morinda citrifolia*, also known as Indian mulberry, the fruit and leaves used in traditional medicine.

Fenghuang: Mythical Chinese bird resembling the peacock.

Beta: Indonesian for "son" or "I."

"As rivers flow into the ocean…": *The Bhagavad Gita*: Chapter 2, Verse 70, translated by Eknath Easwaran.

Chapter 4

Pela: Indonesian for "brother."

Dangdut koplo: Regional music genre distinguished by its arrangements, special drum pattern, up-tempo, and erotic form of dancing.

"...war with the Fretilin and the Democratic Union...": The Fretilin (*Frente Revolucionária de Timor-Leste Independente,* or Revolutionary Front for an Independent East Timor) and Timorese Democratic Union (*União Democrática Timorense*) were the main political parties in East Timor. Soon after the referendum for independence was passed, Indonesia-backed paramilitaries and soldiers carried out a campaign of violence on the island, resulting in over 2000 deaths.

Chapter 5

Puing: Indonesian for "debris."

Idul Fitri: Indonesian Muslim holiday when workers return to their home villages or cities and ask forgiveness from their families.

Bael tree: *Aegle marmelos,* also known as Bengal quince, bears fruit with a hard, woody shell.

Ketapang tree: *Terminalia catappa,* also known as Malabar almond, with large leaves and grows to a height of one hundred feet or more.

Antanan: *Centella asiatica,* commonly known in the West as centella, an herbaceous plant used in various traditional medicines.

Terlalu Manis: Indonesian for "too sweet."
Assalamu alaikum: Muslim phrase meaning, "peace be upon you."

Chapter 6

Banyan Tree Party: Suharto's Golkar Party, whose logo was a banyan tree.
Village Consultative Board: *Lembaga Musyawarah Desa,* the LMD.
Village Community Resilience Board: *Lembaga Ketahan Masyarakat Desa*, the LKMD.
Ibu: Respectful term of address for an older woman, meaning "mother."
"If I speak…": 1 Corinthians 13:1
Salat prayers: A series of prayers said at five different times during the day, preceded by ablutions.
Bagea: Snack made from sago and wrapped in palm leaves.

Chapter 8

"rats that suddenly appear…": From a poem by Goenawan Mohamad.

Chapter 9

Ken sa faak: The literal translation is "two and two are always four." Kei philosophy based on human fallibility, meaning both sides have faults and virtues and these should be recognized and admitted.
"Love is patient…": I Corinthians 13:4–8a

Dailokoh: *Urena lobata,* known in Indonesian as Pulutan, and English as Caesar weed.

Ladeh: *Timonius timon,* with round fruit similar to a crab apple.

Galatoda: *Leea indica,* known in Indonesian as Girang merah or Mali-mali, and English as Bandicoot berry.

Gwaya: *Macaranga tanarius,* known in Indonesian as Mara, and English as Hairy mahang.

Posi-posi: *Sonneratia alba,* known in Indonesian as Perepat, and English as Mangrove apple.

Gumrucai: *Cassytha filiformis,* known in Indonesian as Tali puteri, and English as Devil's gut.

Balacai: *Jatropha curcas,* known in Indonesian as Jarak Pagar, and English as Barbados nut.

Binahong: *Bassela Rubra Linn,* known in English as Heartleaf Maderavine Madevine.

Sife siflyoi: A traditional game for girls.

Larat: Indonesian root word for miserable, *melarat.*

Chapter 11

Hong bird: Chinese bird similar to the phoenix, symbolizing miracles.

Wayang: Shadow play, originally from Java.

Kleine Schoolatlas Van Nederlandsch Oost Indie, Denhaag Weltevreden: Small School Atlas of the Dutch East Indies, The Hague, Weltevreden, 1927.

Chapter 12

Nevnev: A violation of Larwul Ngabal.

Chapter 17

"We are what we think…": *The Dhammapada*, Chapter 1, Verse 1, translated by Eknath Easwaran.

Chapter 18

"…in the movie, *Lupus*.": Indonesian film directed by Achiel Nasrun in 1987.

Insha'Allah: God willing.

Chapter 19

Ambon Manise : Sweet Ambon, in Ambonese.

Ketapang incident: In November 1998, a turf war over control of a parking lot sparked a riot in Ketapang, North Jakarta. It quickly escalated into a conflict between Christians and Muslims after rumors spread that a mosque had been burned down.

Maghrib: Muslim evening praying time, just after sunset.

Chapter 20

Several Muslims are killed: This attack prompted a retaliation on December 11, 2001, in which a ship carrying Christians was bombed at the Galala port in Ambon. A follow-up attack by the Reds resulted in the burning of the Ambon City Council building.

Kolak: A sweet, syrupy dish.

"…peace ceremony held in Tual…": The tribal chief throws four palm fronds in the four wind directions: north, south, east, and west. This signifies that the ritual is fully accepted on all sides. Once the fronds are thrown, a prohibition is in place and there must be no more bloodshed.

About the Author

Born in Lipulalongo, a small village of clove growers in Central Sulawesi, Erni Aladjai earned her degree in French literature from the Hasannudin University in Makassar, Sulawesi. She has worked as a journalist in Makassar, was also a news editor, and managed a learning institution. Erni is currently a full time writer and freelance fiction editor. Local as well as national media have published several of her poems, essays, and short stories. Her novel, *Kei,* took first place in the 2011 Jakarta Arts Council novel competition. Other award-winning works include "*Sampo Soie Soe, Si Juru Masak (Sampo Soie Soe, the Cook)*" at the 2012 Jakarta International Literary Festival. Her two novellas, *Rumah Perahu (The Houseboat)* and *Sebelum Hujan di Seasea (Before the Rain in Seasea),* took second and third place in the 2011 *Cerber Femina* awards. Erni is also the author of the novels *Pesan Cinta dari Hujan (The Promise of Love from the Rain,* Insist Press, 2010) and *Ning di Bawah Gerhana (Ning Under the Eclipse,* Bumen Pustaka Emas, 2013).

More Storytellers from

Dalang Publishing

Only a Girl
Lian Gouw

Three generations of Chinese women struggle for identity against a political backdrop of the World Depression, World War II, and the Indonesian Revolution. Nanna, the matriarch of the family, strives to preserve the family's traditional Chinese values while her children are eager to assimilate into Dutch colonial society. Carolien, Nanna's youngest daughter, is fixated on the advantages to be gained by adopting a western lifestyle. Jenny's western upbringing puts her at a disadvantage in the newly independent Indonesian state where Dutch culture is no longer revered. The unique ways in which Nanna, Carolien, and Jenny face their own challenges reveal the complexity of Chinese society in Indonesia between 1930 and 1952.

Price: $17.95
Paperback: 298 pages
ISBN: 978-0-9836273-7-1

My Name is Mata Hari
Remy Sylado
English rendition by Dewi Anggraeni

My Name is Mata Hari tells the story of the infamous dancer and courtesan who began as Margaretha Geertruida Zelle, a young Dutch woman who married the older Rudolph MacLeod, a military officer, and traveled with him to the Dutch East Indies. Claiming her mother's Javanese ancestry, she changed her name to Mata Hari, Malay for "eye of the day."

Mata Hari danced on stages across Europe and the Middle East, and took many high-ranking military and government officials as her lovers. At the end of a tumultuous life, convicted for espionage during the First World War yet sustained by her pride, she said, "I am a genuine courtesan. And I am a dancer in the true sense."

Price: $17.95
Paperback: 334 pages
ISBN: 978-0-9836273-0-2

***

Potions and Paper Cranes
Lan Fang
English translation by Elisabet Titik Murtisari

In Lan Fang's award-winning novel, Sulis is a young woman selling potions in Surabaya's harbor district. She meets Sujono, a day laborer with dreams of becoming a freedom fighter, and whose passion for Matsumi, a geisha called to Java by a Japanese general, is destined to ruin all of them. Each tells the story of their lives during the Japanese occupation of Java and Indonesia's transition from a Dutch colony to an independent republic.

Price: $17.95
Paperback: 252 pages
ISBN: 978-0-9836273-3-3

Daughters of Papua
Anindita Siswanto Thayf
English translation by Stefanny Irawan

Pum is a loyal old dog who can smell colors. Along with Kwee, a pig with attitude, and seven-year-old Leksi, they tell the story of Mabel. As a young girl of the Dani tribe born and raised in Papua's interior, Dutch missionaries take her to the city under the pretense of adopting her. Mabel quickly adapts to being domestic help and is eager to learn, but her request to attend school is denied: "You know enough and learning too much will only harm you." When Mabel eventually returns to her village years later, her daughter-in-law and granddaughter, Leksi, join her.

The women work in the fields all day long, and Mabel sells the fruits and vegetables from their labor in the open market. Living in Papua is a battle between tradition and the new: for the Papuan people this means leaving the land and working in the gold mining operation on the Holy Mountain, home of the spirits of the Amungme people. The mining company takes the labor from many Papuans and only gives riches to very few. Mabel holds on to the traditional way of life, and dares to speak out against injustice during a fierce election.

Price: $17.95
Paperback: 202 pages
ISBN: 978-0-9836273-9-5